Being the account of inexplicable events recorded by Wilfred Trevy Farquhar begun in the year of our Lord, 1888.

CHARLES GAR ROPER, Ph.D,
December, 2012
Freeport, Maine

Copyright © 2013 Charles Gar Roper, Ph.D,
All rights reserved.
ISBN: 097682762X
ISBN 13: 9780976827627

Acknowledgements:

I am deeply grateful to many people for many reasons for helping to bring Tales of the Traveler into the world.

To my daughter, Jane Roper, who read the first story and told me it made her imagine a whole series of stories woven together in some sort of anthology. To my wife, Betsy Eckert Roper, the "Irish girl" who reads what I write and is unfailingly honest, guiding me with her insightful feedback and careful attention to detail and continuity.

I thank Grael Norton of Wheatmark Publishing who coached my writing and gave me invaluable help. A tip of the hat, too, to the Great Courses series and Professor Brooks Landon, University of Iowa, whose sanction of my rather obvious belief that a good sentence is not always the shortest, simplest, most succinct, bare-bones damn sentence, recharged my confidence.

Thanks are due to the many *citizens of the world* who opened their homes and lives to me as I made my own travels through England, Ireland, Scotland and Europe. Their histories, stories and DNA are bred into the people who inhabit *this* traveler's tales. In the same way, I give thanks to Leo Katz and other OMNI Camp staff and kids who came from Russia and introduced me to a remarkable national personality as well as the delightful cadence of their language.

Finally, I thank Sam Hunneman and Maryellen Carew. Sam, my Editor, made a thousand suggestions for wording, phrasing, description and language, of which 999 were utter perfection. That other suggestion was pretty good also. Her help with dialect, action and texture cannot be over-emphasized. Maryellen, who was charged with creating our cover, sat patiently waiting for the muse to visit, and then, in collaboration with this blithe spirit, created the perfect combination of visual appeal and symbolically moving art which simply says it all.

Editors Note: The following work offers publication of the journal of my great-great-uncle, Wilfred Trevy Farquhar, lately discovered among his papers.

The journal is reproduced here exactly as written. Any errors are those in the original. As Editor, I make no judgment as to the truth of these tales, but only present them here for the reader's consideration.

- C. G. Roper – 2012

~Prologue~

Since I no longer pursued my chosen profession, having given up medicine two years before, I guess I would, at the time, have simply called myself a traveler. My young wife had died in the spring of 1886, thereby crushing our dream of aging together through the turn of the century. We had not been blest with children.

My older brother was lost, either at sea or in the jungles of Panama in 1880, while traveling to California in pursuit of gold. My parents had also died prematurely, after surviving the horrors of the Civil War and even prospering in the years thereafter, they passed within six months of one another, only in their mid-fifties, a scant year before I lost my darling wife. Little wonder that I found myself in the deepest reaches of despair.

So it was that I had lost my purpose in life, and viewing all those who claimed to find theirs in religion, work, or even family, as fools living in self-deception, I no longer considered myself capable of administering the healing arts, which require a solid footing in both science and faith. I had, within in my soul, no confidence in either kind of knowing.

I decided, therefore, to set out on a journey that I hoped would bring me back to a focus on life and the living, after so much death in such a short time. Armed with a leather-bound travel journal and a newfangled invention called a Kodak Film Camera, I embarked on an open-ended journey to try to fill the black, empty chambers of loss which my heart had become. So dark were my inner thoughts that I secretly imagined—even hoped—that the ship upon which I traveled would be overtaken by storms and sink, taking me with it into peaceful oblivion.

My crossing, however, was uneventful, and I landed in Glasgow, Scotland, which port I had chosen based on a quite arbitrary purpose; to visit the home places of my ancestral family. To that end, I traveled from Glasgow to Edinburgh, arriving on the last Monday in February in the year 1888.

Fig. 1: The Kodak Film Camera sent to me from the Kodak Company by my friend, George Eastman, the inventor, in 1888; one of three he sent out in this way. He asked me to give the device a trial run as he intended to soon release it for the general public. I had no particular interest in photography, but agreed to take it on my journey. As it turned out, it was a quite marvelous addition to the whole experience, and I heartily recommend it to others.

~I~
Balmoral, Scotland - March 8th, 1888

I took lodgings in Edinburgh at the McCranmen Inn, a grey stone affair of some antiquity, but finding the room cramped and the food suitable only for creatures less civilized than swine, I decided to move on to Crathie in Aberdeenshire, to look about in the area of Balmoral Castle which was the historic home of my Farquhar family, then called McFarquharson, or sometimes simply Farquar.

The Blanenbar House, a rambling country inn surrounded by a low wall and garden, provided me accommodation with a large, clean bedchamber, and had as well, a lively pub boasting a well-staffed kitchen run by one Mrs. Drummond, whose scones alone might have given me reason to carry on.

Thoroughly exhausted after an endless, jostling, rain-drenched carriage ride out of Edinburgh, I retired early on the Thursday night of my arrival. By the next morning, the weather had cleared, but I put off going up to the castle, assuming it to be occupied by the King and his family and therefore viewed only from some distance, and spent my time walking about the village instead.

My impression was that Crathie, with its neat shops and well-kempt cottage residences all nestled close together, was a friendly village, as witnessed by the willingness of the village folk to strike up a conversation with such as myself. I had, by late afternoon, learned quite a bit of lore regarding my family in the area round about.

The stuff of local legend, the Farquhars were described to me as having been large people and fierce warriors. But over time, consistently and foolishly putting themselves at the fore of screaming charges against their enemies, while other supporting clans followed behind, their numbers were greatly reduced. In the earliest days, I was told, they fought completely naked. I daresay that my imagination quaked at this image, and it was difficult to choose whether that or their later fighting style with painted faces, waving kilts, and pipes blaring like the unearthly screech of banshees, would have been more frightening.

In any case, I came to understand that in the years from the 1500's through the early 1700's, the Farquharsons had held powerful sway over this region, controlling huge sections of land which included both

Braemar and Balmoral Castles. This power wavered, however, during and after the political difficulties in 1745, and the later financial ones in 1848 when the clan was forced to turn over Balmoral Castle to Queen Victoria.

When I returned to the pub, the barkeep, upon my telling him of my quest for family roots, showed me an old painting hanging over the bar, portraying an event entitled, "The Gathering of the Clan Farquhar." He described the picture in detail, pointing to each figure as his jaw worked vigorously, animating his heavy jowls and mutton chop burnsides.

The picture showed a great banquet with a host of kilt-clad clansmen feasting on roast pig, and drinking and toasting from great wooden chalices. The women shown were much in the background, but several dark-haired beauties in long gowns were pictured, looking attentively to their lairds' needs. Also shown were lute players and pipers, festooned with feathers, and beside a large man seated upon a raised dais, there lay an enormous gray wolfhound. I found that the picture exerted a strong pull on my feelings.

Taking my glass of beer from the bar, I retired to a rough-hewn table with a bench behind it stationed against the wall, where I would have a good point of observation for the room. Now a certain man dressed in ordinary country fashion came in and was greeted in a friendly and familiar fashion by the barman. I saw this, but only incidentally, and took no real notice of him until, as he stood at the bar and struck up a bit of talk with the barman, I became aware that the two were pointing to the same picture of my ancestral gathering, and that as they spoke, the stranger gestured, first to the picture and then to me. So I was not altogether surprised, but perhaps a bit disquieted when this fellow turned from the bar and, carrying his pint with him, approached my table.

"So it's Farquhar then?" he addressed me. "May I join ye?" and sat himself down before I could either assent or decline.

He proceeded to look me straight in the eye, not in the manner of a stranger, but rather as if he were an old acquaintance who had been expecting me, and even that we were making the connection that had been intended by my having come into the town in the first place.

"So ye *will* be going wi' me to the castle tomorrow in the afternoon," he stated.

"I-I beg your pardon," I stammered, to which he replied, "Ye'll be wantin' to visit Balmoral, I wager," and I had to confess that that was, in fact, my intention, but could not stop myself from asking rather rudely, in what way it was a matter of regard to him.

At this point he offered an apology, "Ah, but o'course. Please forgive me, I didna introduce m'self. I'm Brian McFrane, him that's the husband of Anne

Farquhar. If Anne were here, she could make the family connection for ye, how ye two must be cousins some many generation's times removed, but I don't follow it well in me own mind, and Anne's wi' us nae longer."

I expressed my sympathies at his wife's demise, but he waved off my respectful tone with the explanation that she'd been gone a long time, to which I felt compelled to add further deferential remarks.

Then he explained that as a Farquhar—by marriage at least—and known to some extent, he had certain access to the castle, which might otherwise be barred, and he offered most graciously to escort me there on Saturday afternoon. As he made the offer, I felt a thrill of excitement quite above the level to be expected at the simple prospect of having a guide to show me about. In fact, I could not quite define the emotion I felt.

We made arrangements to meet there in the pub at three o'clock the next day, and I returned to my quarters at Blanenbar House where I found, after I retired to my bed, that I could not sleep for an agitated anticipation of the morrow's visit. As far as the gentleman knowing of my intent and wishes, I put it down to my many conversations about the village regarding my search of family legends.

I arrived in the pub early the next day and was sitting over a pint, when the stranger, or more correctly now, my newly discovered—if distant—relative, Brian

McFrane arrived. He was dressed in walking clothes, knickers and high socks, a tweed jacket, and a hunter's cap. I was in twill slacks with a blue jacket over, and felt that surely I stuck out as an American on holiday, my overcoat being cut in a distinctly American fashion.

Brian offered his hand and surprised me by clasping, not my hand, but my forearm, and giving a very vigorous embrace in that manner.

Leaving my drink unfinished, I hurried out at Brian's urging, and together we walked from the village to the lane that wound its way out to the grounds of Balmoral. It was a long way, and because the land was heavily treed, I did not glimpse the castle until, all of a sudden, we brought up before a large iron gate, through which the magnificent edifice spread up and out before us.

At the gate stood a royal guard, solemn and seemingly unmoving, for although I saw not so much as the flick of a finger, some system of counterbalanced weights was triggered as we approached, and the gate swung open. Brian McFrane turned to me as we passed through the royal protections and winked, "Ye see," he said, "I do have a certain access," then, walking on toward the castle, he smiled at me in a way that was both conspiratorial and friendly.

At the front door, one of many portals facing the courtyard, a second guard stood similarly erect and unblinking. As before, the door swung open at our approach. Brian then guided me along a corridor off the reception hall, striding ahead with a clear indication that he knew exactly where to go. Midway down the corridor we came to a pair of large wooden doors, arched in a gothic curve, and there we stopped. From behind the doors came the sounds of raucous laughter, shouting, and music from stringed instruments. Brian suggested I stand a step back as he raised a fisted hand to pound heavily on the door.

From within came a booming voice, "Enter and hail, brothers!" Whereupon Brian grasped the large iron door rings and turning them together, clearly familiar with their workings, pushed open the doors.

Inside, a wondrous sight accosted me. An enormous long table heaped with food and surrounded by men, all clad in kilts, who stood or sat or even lay around and across the table. The din in the room was great, a combination of merriment and music, accented from time to time with the clash of broad swords, one against another, in what appeared to be friendly jousting, not actual combat. The music swelled to a louder pitch as pipers joined in.

Brian led me to the table where he reached out and, in the manner he had done with me earlier, grasped the forearm of the enormous man standing at its head. They spoke in a language which was harsh yet melodic, with words I did not understand. This man, clad as he was in full kilt and Highland regalia, complete with badger sporran and a richly bejeweled crest pin at his shoulder, appeared to be the leader. Indeed, as Brian made our introductions, he indicated that this was the "Chief."

This Chief turned and spoke to me, still in words I did not understand until Brian translated them, "Ye are most welcome here, Farquhar, son of Farquhar."

I answered with a thank you and then turned, bewildered, to Brian. "What is this then? A reenactment or a reunion?"

"Something o'the sort I guess ye could call it," he answered, to which I replied, "How incredibly fortuitous!" Brian said that it was more a matter of fate than fortune, which remark I did not fully understand.

Then I was led to a rack on the side wall where hung two voluminous sashes in the same tartan as the collected revelers wore, with a crest pin I recognized as the Farquhar crest, stating *Fide et Fortitudine*, Faith and Fortitude. Brian donned his ample sash, and I was amused—even somewhat relieved as I felt a bit foolish in my contemporary American dress—when he indicated that I should put on the other.

More suitably dressed, Brian walked to two chairs, well down the great table, where we took seats and immediately thereupon, young women, full-bosomed to overflowing their bodices, came and filled our cups with wine. This was followed by a great heaped plate of meat, both pig and duck. There being no forks but only a dagger at each place, I watched, and then copied Brian as he stabbed great hunks of meat and gnawed them. Our cups seemed to empty quickly, and were as quickly refilled by the girls who smiled at us as they brushed back their long hair which fell sometimes in plaits and sometimes hanging long down their backs; some blond, some red-headed, some with midnight-black tresses.

The meal continued until the Chief stood and commanded silence, then for a long period, he spoke—I should say recited, a rhythmic oration, not one word of which I understood but for the occasional sound of the name Farquhar. When he had finished, the company stood as one and raised their cups in a toast before many took partners onto the floor for dancing; wild jigs and also martial music that I would have imagined giving rise to marching, but instead caused these couples to leap and lunge.

It soon became evident from the stumbling and falling, that the company was indeed becoming very drunk. Some couples retired to the sides of the hall, where I looked but turned quickly away when I saw rather bold and bawdy unlacing of dresses and eager hands running up beneath skirts and kilts.

I did not join in the merry dancing, but did accept several kisses from one of the serving girls who had taken a notion to sit upon my lap, hanging on my neck and talking to me in that strange tongue. I was, by now, quite drunk myself, the hour being very late and the drinks being many. I turned to Brian to request that he escort me home, whereupon he stood and reminded me that I owed my host thanks and good-bye.

On rather unsteady legs, I approached the Chief and bowing, thanked him. He thrust his arm toward me and taking mine in his mighty grasp, held me long in that manner. Then he released me and with his fist, thumped three times on his heart, followed each time with a gesture toward me. From his belt, he drew forth a dagger which aroused in me substantial, if momentary, alarm. The weapon was an intricately ornate work with the Farquhar crest upon it, and the Chief made clear that I was to take it as a gift. His eyes were filled with something that struck me as perhaps pride, and seemed even to be gazing on me with love.

I bowed again and turned to Brian who, having once more clasped and released the Chief's arm, walked me back to the great doors where we had entered. There we stopped and he asked if I might be able to find my way back to my rooms by myself, as he intended to stay and sleep with the company *in situ*. Already, many had drawn out pallets to lie down upon and were pulling their cloaks about them. Although I felt a good bit clouded in my mind from drink, I assured Brian that I could find my way.

I returned to the inn without incident, passing by the guards who opened the gates as before, giving me not a glance. In my room, I collapsed onto my bed and slept the sleep of strong intoxication.

I did not awaken until nearly noon the next day, and after partaking of a small luncheon, because my head still pounded and my stomach roiled, I determined to return to the castle to find Brian and thank him for a most extraordinary evening. I took along the camera, in order that I might correct the error I had made in not bringing it the evening before.

I dithered along the path, lurching just a bit from time to time, rubbing my eyes every so often to try to restore some better clarity to them and to my mind also. I arrived at the great iron gate that stood before the courtyard and lifted my hand in a brief salute to the guard standing there, not expecting, but certainly hoping, that he might recognize me from the afternoon before, as I had determined he was the same man.

He moved not at all.

Still, I waited for the gate to open and when it did not, I approached and explained myself, invoking Brian McFrane's name and recounting my visit of the preceding evening.

The guard, his face fixed in a most questioning expression, now spoke, "Ye say ye were here yesterday e'nin' and attended a gathering of your clan? Ye say ye were in the castle? Ye say ye came wi' this Brian McFrane?"

I was becoming somewhat exasperated as his questions had a ring of repetitive obtuseness. I answered as politely as I could that he had stated the matter most accurately.

"Not possible," he spat at me. "An' just what sort o'misadventure are ye trying to accomplish here, sir?"

His words shocked me and I quickly answered that indeed, I intended no misdeed at all, and what, I asked, gave him to say that my visit, which I knew to have been most definitely the truth, was impossible?

"Because," he said, his color rising, his eyes nearly bulging from their sockets, "this castle was unoccupied last night. The King and his company had quit residence yestermorn and returned to London. The house was closed and draped, leaving only the guards and a few house staff."

I implored him to allow me to enter, but he said that under no circumstances could that be permitted.

Fig. 2: Balmoral Castle, photographed the day after my evening there, when I had regrettably neglected to take my camera.

Wandering then back to the bar, I sought out the publican and asked him about his patron, Brian McFrane, and what he might know of the reenactment, or at least the gathering of Farquhars, at the castle. He looked at me in a strange manner and informed me that he had had no customer by name of McFrane, nor did he know of anyone by that name in the district nearby.

I referred him to the picture hanging above the bar, of which he and Brian, and indeed, he and I had lately spoken. To my astonishment, the picture now hanging, contained within the familiar fame, showed not the gathering of a clan—Farquhar or any other—but rather, the gathering of a flock! In place of kilted Scotts, there appeared a tumult of sheep being directed into a pen, guarded and directed by two farmers and their dogs. Most of the flock piled forward in disarray, leaping and lunging, while two pairs stood to the side, rutting, and one lone beast, cut off from the rest by the dogs, looked on, bleating in bewilderment.

Calling this strange substitution to the attention of the barkeep, he winked and said, "Weel, I'll guess ye had a wee bit too much of our good Scottish drink last night."

I stayed only one day more in Crathie making more inquiries to try to reconcile the facts that I knew to be true concerning the gathering at the castle, but consistently met with blank looks or vigorous denials from all with whom I spoke. In short, I could find no verification, yet I could neither explain nor deny that I now had in my possession an ornate dagger bearing the Farquhar crest, that precious gift from the Chief of the Clan Farquhar. My Chief.

Fig. 3: A drawing from memory of the appearance of one of the men gathered in the castle. I regretted that I had not taken my camera.

~II~
Yorkshire, England – March 24th, 1888

From the church records:

John Thornborough, Knight of Thornborough,
Yorkshire, c. 1170 – 1214
Son: William de Thornburgh, Knight, Yorkshire,
1210 – 1253
Son: William de Thornburgh, Knight, Yorkshire,
1250 – 1289

※

Son: Robert Thornborough, Yorkshire,
c. 1661 – 1715
Son: Walter Thornburgh, Pennsylvania,
1711 - 1783
Son: Edward Thornburgh, Virginia,
1741 – 1790

Still in pursuit my ancient family connections, I traveled from Crathie, south to Thirsk in Yorkshire, and there found that a town existed, as I had heard from my uncle, bearing the name of my Grandmother's family, that being Thornborough (Pronounced ***Thorn****-brah*, sometimes spelled Thornburgh). The town lay only nine miles from Thirsk and was thus an easy ride by carriage.

Having arranged to hire the suitable rig and driver, I set off of an early morning and enjoyed the fine air as we trotted down the narrow lane to the village. Finding there no public house at which to make inquiries, I decided to be bold and simply knock at the door of a well-set house with an inviting garden before it. The door was opened by a woman of middle age to whom I gave a slight bow and quickly explained that my family bore in its lineage, the name Thornborough, and that I sought to discover if I might trace these roots back to some original family of Thornboroughs.

In answer, she told me that to her knowledge there lived no family of that name in the village, but upon taking a moment more to think, she suggested that I inquire of the family who lived in a very old house of sizeable proportions on the large farm outside of the village center, possibly once called "Thornborough Farm." She kindly gave me directions, and remounting my carriage, I instructed the driver to take me hence.

The house to which I had been directed lay at the end of a long tree-lined lane, well-fenced, with greening fields of spring crops growing on either side. Painted a cheerful yellow, the house contrasted with most of the other structures of the region which were, with few exceptions, made of brown stone. The house appeared to be in excellent condition, and the very thick walls which were revealed at the window spaces did indeed suggest that it was a house of some antiquity. There were, standing close to the house, several large stone barns, as well as the ruins of several other outbuildings that further reinforced the sense that this was a very old estate indeed.

I knocked at the door and heard inside an explosion of sound; a number of barking dogs who came in a rush to stand, scratching and growling on the other side. Some moments later, the door was opened and dogs' bodies swarmed around me, turning me several times 'round before I could catch my balance. As the dogs' uproar settled to muted yapping and sniffing, I was able to see a young woman, perhaps in her early thirties, who stood wiping her hands with a dish towel. The rush of dogs seemed to strike her as nothing of note, and she made no excuse or apology.

Feeling ill at ease and not knowing what to say, I simply put forth the question, "Do you know if this farm may have been an original estate or manor of Thornborough?" I asked, quickly adding that Thornborough was a surname in my family lineage.

The woman smiled and answered "Oh, but truly I dinna know." Then she called out in the direction of the barn, "Grandfather. A visitor with a question for ye."

Almost immediately, an old man came walking in, carrying a milking can and shaking his head. He fixed his eyes on me as he approached, and then coming up quite close, he reprimanded me in a gruff voice, "Yon cow needs to be milked. She'll not long continue to gi' milk if she is neglected."

I felt at a loss as to how to respond, but the woman quickly assured him, "Grandfather, I shall speak to Daniel about it, but please, a moment. Do ye know aught of this farm's history and of a family named Thornborough who may have lived here?"

Gruffly, the old man answered, "I dinna know the name but 'tis what we call the town and lands here about," and turned to go, quite rudely and without further comment. Or perhaps, I thought, he is quite deaf.

I was disappointed that there appeared to be no easy memory to make the connection to a particular family who may have given the name to the town, but before I could thank the old man and his granddaughter, he turned back and spoke again, mayhap a bit less suspiciously.

"If ye would speak to Old John Tars, now living in Masham, nae far from here, he may have a word for ye. He lived here in Thornborough and is a good deal older than I and may know summat might help ye."

"How," I asked "might I locate John Tars?"

The old man responded with a deep chuckle and a smile, "You need only ask of any man, woman or bairn in Masham, for ever'one knows John Tars."

It being early in the day, I asked my driver if he might be able to stay with me and continue the journey to Masham. He agreed, having no other service reserved, and adding that he would be most glad of the extra income.

We arrived at our destination in the early afternoon; still in time for—and much in need of—lunch, and went into to a likely free house in the town's center. Feeling a bit foolish, I inquired of the young man serving us as to whether he knew the whereabouts of John Tars.

"Aye, I most certainly do. He lives on't farm wi' me father, who is John Tars' great-great-great-grandson, as I, ye see, am his great-great-great-great-grandson!"

Thinking the young man must be quite befuddled concerning generations, I thanked him for this intelligence and started to put forward a question, "As you appear to me to be a man of no great age . . . "

"I am thirty and eight."

"Ah . . . then I may presume that your father is perhaps near sixty?"

Smiling, the young man corrected me, "He is, in truth, seventy-two."

With my mind beginning to riot, I pressed further, "But how then could John Tars be your father's great-great-great-grandfather?"

"How then, indeed?" the man answered. "And how old then do ye reckon John Tars to be?"

As I struggled to calculate the math of generations, this Tars descendent told me, "John Tars is presently, as best we can determine, one hundred and fifty-two years old. My father and I are all that remains of his line, since my father's father and grandfather have both passed before."

"So you mean to say that if this age be actual, the current year being 1888," I struggled to form the words, "that would mean that John Tars was born in or about 1736?"

I did the rough math in my head, allowing twenty years for each generation beyond the age of this young man and his father, though even that seemed perhaps to underestimate John Tars' date of birth by some years, given the fact that men in those times were usually past thirty when they married.

Now, more curious and dumbfounded that ever, I inquired if it might be possible to visit the old man.

"He would, I believe, be most pleased. And if ye will tolerate it, he will insist in filling ye with stories which remain bright in his mind in spite of his advanced age. Our farm is only a mile or so from here, and as I am finished this afternoon wi' my work here, I would be happy to take ye there."

We arrived at the farm which was called "Twitchell Fence" according to the old chiseled stone by the gate. The farm house was a modest stone structure, and white smoke was rising out of the chimney making a welcoming appearance. William, as I had learned his name to be, directed me to the door, then without rapping, opened it, calling out as he did, "Hallo! Hey there, Grandfather John, ye have a visitor."

It was in fact not John who greeted me, but a woman who quickly introduced herself as Evelyn. I presumed her to be William's mother, and she appeared to be somewhat over fifty years of age, still younger than William had said of his father. She smiled broadly and waved me in saying, "Have a sit wi' Himself by the fire while I put on the kettle. And Will, go and fetch in the coachman. Poor bugger must be feeling the chill as the afternoon settles in."

With an outstretched hand, she directed me toward a large, straight-backed wooden chair set by the fire, across from which, in a chair much more comfortably designed, reclined a very old man. He did, in fact, look ancient; his face wizened, his beard long but straggly, his hair a comic clump upon his pate, his smile a travesty of toothlessness, with his thin shoulders wrapped in a shawl.

I could not say if I had expected such an ancient one to look younger or older, never having seen nor even heard of anyone of such advanced age, but I noted that his eyes were bright and clear, aglow with a merriness about them that lit up his expression at my coming.

"Sit, sit," he said, as though I had not already taken the seat. "Do ye wish a smoke?" Whereupon he took out a curved pipe from beneath his shawl and proceeded to pinch several packings of tobacco from a box that was set on the table beside him; filling, tamping, then finally lighting the bowl with a long wooden match.

Also on the table lay several volumes, one of substantial heft, which titles I could not make out. The top book, handsomely leather-bound, was turned over opened, no doubt put down in interruption of reading. Striking a second match, John Tars continued to address me, "What lore may ye be seeking, lad?" Adding, rather under his breath, " . . . since that seems to be the occasion for most of my visits of late."

I congratulated him on his perspicacity and confessed that I did indeed seek some lore; that being information about my family, named Thornborough, of the village which I guessed was named for some old forbearer.

"Nay, young man, ye're quite in error." The old man stopped then, and I was taken quite aback by his abruptness, as well as the negative assertion. Did he mean I was mistaken to ask him for this information, or that I was mistaken about the family connection? Not knowing how to continue the conversation, I sat, holding my tongue as the old man took several deep draws upon his pipe, then blew the smoke toward the ceiling, a look of great satisfaction upon his face.

"See, the family is named for the town," he said, breaking the silence, "not t'other way 'round. Thornborough refers to the thorn bushes on the hills there, hence the town is called Thornborough, from ancient tongue and times, ye see. The site dates back at least to the Druids and has yet today the remains of the stone circle monuments."

I was struck dumb, astounded by this lesson so clearly stated. And the old man had more to tell.

"Now ye need not be discouraged as I can tell ye of the family, even how it came to be that they traveled to America, whence I presume you yourself have come. Y'see, when I was a boy, born and raised in Thornborough, there was a lady, daughter of Robert Thornborough, and she remained in the village with her mother after Robert deserted them and went off to find his fortune. We heard he later remarried in the Colonies, did Robert, and had two sons, Walter and Edward.

"The family had suffered terribly, ye see, during the years of the Glorious Revolution which saw King James II overthrown and the religious tolerance he had asserted undone by William the Orange. The cruelty of those times didna touch me personally, and I only learnt of those wicked times when they were taught to me in school, some seventy years after the Jacobites fell.

"But so it was that young Thornborough gave up his lands and title, abandoned his wife and daughter, and sailed away in the last of the century, 1698, fleeing the religious conflict that so besieged Scotland, particularly the Highlands, for generations. Aye, he abandoned everything, seeking freedom in the Colonies of America.

"After 'er mother died, only Margaret remained. She had married Thomas Coswain, and though she'd three children—not counting the twa that died as infants—the Thornborough name, in direct line and connected to the village, was done.

"Now it 'appened that Maggie, as she was called, set up a kind of school for those village children who were of a mind to want to learn to read, and I being among the number, came to have this advantage, as well as a great deal of information that she shared wi' us about the history o' the town and the region; in particular as it related to her family, dating back to the days of William the Conqueror and the very first Thornborough who was William de Thornborough, so named as he was knighted and granted a coat of arms by King Edward I."

I sat listening with my mouth open, my tea growing cold where it perched upon my knee.

Suddenly, with a great laugh, Old John winked at me with a hint of what I could only describe as lust, before continuing his memories.

"Did I tell ye," he went on, "that Maggie Thornborough had children? Or mention that one was

Helen, and that it was Helen I courted and married in 1777? Aye, so my wife was Helen Coswain, the granddaughter of Robert Thornborough."

So astounded was I at all of this that I stood and began to pace, unable to contain my rush of excitement and wonder. Here I met with a stranger, only a brief acquaintance, a man one hundred and fifty-two years of age, who had known— indeed had married - someone of my direct lineage, more than one hundred years ago.

For some while then, John held sway, speaking of the foolishness of the American Revolution, and the tragedy of the French Revolution, and the defeat of Napoleon, the expansion of the British Empire, the movement against slavery, and of course, the Great American Civil War. His knowledge was encyclopedic and he treated it all as though he were reporting the news of the day.

The hour having grown late, I begged to excuse myself, and with many expressions of appreciation, took my leave.

Driving back to Thirsk, I pondered all that I had experienced, and came to find, in the incredible longevity of John Tars, a greater appreciation of history seen in such large bites, as well as a profound and marvelous sense of human progress through time.

~III~
Cornwall, England – April 16th, 1888

So puzzled was I after my encounters at Balmoral and Thornborough, that after several days of travel down to the southwest of England to the region known as Cornwall, which journey afforded me time for pondering and contemplation, the thought occurred to me that perhaps my experience was not as singular as I might imagine. What if I were to search among the folk in the towns and burghs as I traveled; could I perhaps find similar tales, and perhaps even stranger occurrences?

With this idea in mind, I began inquiring of the people I met if they knew or had heard of inexplicable things, either through local legend or that they had experienced. I was soon rewarded with tales and memories of many events that could not be explained by reason, logic, or experience. I decided then that I would record as many of these *word-of-mouth* tales as I could, with the only criteria for inclusion in my compilation being verification, in the sense that the same, or a very similar tale, was told by multiple persons.

One such legend came to me from the very distant past, but with such consistency in its narrations that I felt sure such an occurrence must have had substance in fact, even if it did not exist within the bounds of normal experience. I first heard the tale from a man I encountered while walking on the high cliffs along the shore above Kynance Cove on the rugged southern coast of Cornwall.

I had stopped to enjoy the view and eat a small lunch which my landlady had packed for me, and as I sat upon a well-placed boulder, this man, a good number of years more advanced in age than myself, came and stood gazing at the sea, directly in front of the spot where I had chosen to pause. I was at first a bit annoyed, preferring my view uninterrupted, and in fact, I was seeking, and much preferred, solitude at this time. After some minutes, I spoke up, asking why he stood just there when there was such a vast expanse of sea cliff to the left and also the right of his chosen spot.

He turned toward me and spoke with a rhythmic cadence reminding me of the sound of epic poems from ancient times, "But do you not know, sir, that on this very spot, King Arthur himself stood and turned the Spanish Armada away from our shores?" He flung an arm toward the sea and continued, "Upon these great cliffs, eight hundred knights, full armor clad, upon their horses mounted, and with banners aloft, streaming in the wind, their armor and lances gleaming in the rays of sun that came shining through the mist, did here present such a fearsome and mighty array, that the Spaniard invaders, battle-ready and lusting for conquest, were filled with such dread that they fell into disarray and turned back, leaving all in peace."

Though no great scholar in the history of the region, I was aware of the Arthurian legend of Camelot and his Knights of the Round Table, reputed to have arisen in the twelfth century in this region of Cornwall, while the event of which the old man spoke—the arrival of the Spanish Armada—to the best of my limited knowledge, was an occurrence of the late 1500's or perhaps early 1600's.

"I do beg your pardon, my good man," I said with as little tone of argumentation as I could manage since I did not wish to offend the old fellow, "but this cannot be. What nature of meaning could I possible attach to such a tale that violates the timeline of history so egregiously?"

"Ah," he sighed, disappointment audible in his voice as he took a deep breath and declared, "You do not understand these things. These men were heroes, and the lives of heroes, their deeds, are not constrained by mortal limits. They exist here in the land where they strode, first as mortals, and as well, in the world of the eternal."

What this man had put forth, I understood, but could not fully embrace. "But," I objected, increasingly incredulous, "how then did these spirits come to present themselves here, four-hundred years after their own time? And to an enemy entirely unknown when they lived?"

Sweeping his raised fist through the air, he quickly continued, paying no heed at all to my doubting tone.

"They were summoned! Summoned by the call to defend what was theirs; what had been passed on to their descendants. They had lived and fought and died to protect England, and so great was the danger sailing in upon the tide with the Spanish fleet, that their spirits rallied, rose from the dust and stood, finding their form and returning to these cliffs, ready to defend their homeland."

"And as you gaze out now, what is it that you look for?" I asked gently, deeply moved by the passion in his voice.

"I seek naught! Look for? Nay, I see! I see the tall ships riding low in the water, showing their great cannons bristling all along their broad sides. I see the lookouts in the rigging and the proud captains on their decks, burning with bravado and confidence. I see them coming closer and closer to shore, men gathering at the rails, scurrying like ants, readying to attack. Hundreds of men. Hundreds of ships. Altogether, numbering thousands."

He was by then trembling with his passion. I asked gently, "Then how could a number so small as eight hundred knights, even if they stood bravely, have turned away such a mighty force."

The old man turned tired eyes back to me and slowly shook his head, "Ach, again you do not understand. Come then and stand with me among them, in their unbroken ranks, full-armed and proud, formed suddenly out of the mist where moments earlier had stood nothing. Stand with me in their silent presence, here where even the clatter of their armor and the shouts of their captains are entombed within a wall of absolute, dead stillness. Feel with me the aura of their bravery, bravery that swelled from gut-deep resolution with such a force that it o'ertook each and every cowardly heart of their would-be conquerors."

But though I stood alongside the old man, I could neither see ships nor feel the battle lines of ancient knights. We remained for some minutes before he turned to me and announced, "They are leaving now," and turned, extending his hand, which I took, accepting his firm grasp as a positive show of friendship.

As he himself turned to go, he assured me, "You will see them yourself one day. If you but trust your senses, and your heart." Then he walked away—briskly, too, I might say—out of sight across the high land.

Though told with great presence and apparent integrity, the tale did not, by these factors alone, qualify to be recorded in my collection according to my own self-imposed requirements that it be thrice-told. Pondering this, I wended my way back across the high plain and down to the village cove where I was staying.

Considering the keeper of the local public house to be, as a rule, a source of broad local knowledge, I approached that man and, as artfully as I could, inquired of him if he knew of an older gentleman whose acquaintance I might have made walking on the cliffs.

"Oh, 'twas Andrew, nae doubt. And did he regale ye concernin' the massin' o'the knights upon the cliff and the turnin' away o'the Spanish Armada?" With this he broke into a broad grin which I took to suggest that the old man's fancy was well known, and a source of local amusement.

Returning the smile, I nodded and said that indeed, it must have been Andrew I had encountered, since he did, in fact, tell me such a tale. I was surprised then, when the barman, now unsmiling to the point of sternness, stated, "Of course, it might ha' been Sara, had ye said 'twas a woman, or John, had ye not said 'old,' for they each tell the story pretty well the same."

Feeling that my criteria of verification might once more be in play, I asked, "And how does it happen that these three each tell the same story?"

"Ye should ask them yourself. They'll each be here this afternoon, I'll allow." Then, once more smiling pleasantly, he turned to his shelf of glasses and began to wipe each one in turn before suddenly turning back to me and asking, "Would ye be wantin' a drink now? Oh, and by the way, the story is a true historical fact."

"How so, historically true?" I asked, now entirely dumbfounded by the barman's comment.

"Oh, 'twas was recorded by the monks in an ancient text from the time of the event, and sure, everyone knows that the armada never landed. Sailed boldly right up to the shore, and then, with never a shot fired, turned and sailed awa' again."

I had him draw me a pint of bitters and withdrew to a table, wondering how I would recognize Sara or John when they came into the pub. Of course I needn't have wondered, since within a few minutes, a woman came in, scanned the room and, spotting me, came straight over to my table.

"Are ye not the traveler who was just this morning up upon the high cliffs?"

I nodded, assenting that I was, and she smiled most attractively. She was a young woman, perhaps twenty-five years of age and dressed, as was the local custom, in a jumper-style dress with apron and full skirt beneath a fitted bodice. Her hair was long and fell in waves down far below her shoulders.

Smiling at me as if in full recognition, she continued, "Aye, I thought as much as ye look the man that

Andrew told me of. And did ye see them there? The knights and their horses?"

I had to admit that I had not seen the vision Andrew described.

"Pity," she said "But ye will . . . that is, if ye go back oftimes enough. Still, they don't come often, and perhaps because ye're not of these parts, ye may not so easily see them."

Now, fully intrigued, I pursued her thought, "And may I presume then, that you *have* seen them?"

"Yes, I have," she told me with pride, "Three times in my life. The first when I was just seven years old, and then not again until I was nineteen. The last time was this spring just passed."

Suddenly aware of my rudeness in not introducing myself, and in having the lady address me while standing by the table like a serving girl, I stood quickly and offered her a chair, "You must be Sara. Please, sit down if you would care to, and I'll order you refreshment."

Without hesitation, she sat down upon the chair I held for her and waved to the barman to bring her drink, which apparently had been expected, as he came 'round the bar carrying a glass of ale already built and delivered it with a flourish.

My eagerness knew no bounds, "Please tell me about your experiences. When you say you have seen 'them,' what is it that you have seen?"

"Why, knights in armor, some mounted on horseback, some afoot." Her answer was given with a slight air suggesting that she thought I must be some sort of simpleton to have asked such a question.

Partly to defend my approach, but mostly out of genuine curiosity, I asked further, "But when you say you saw them, do you mean as a vision or a dream . . . something formed in the sea mist?"

"No mist, nor ghost neither," she decried, now just a bit annoyed. "These be men in fact; strong and fair, their armor cold and glinting in the sun enough to hurt the eye. Horses, hot and breathing heavy in great puffs of steam. With my own hand have I felt the horses' flanks as I walked among them," adding with a wink, "I'm no fool to walk behind a horse without touching the hindquarters to let him know I'm there, ye ken?"

"Do they speak to you? The knights?"

"Nah, nowt t' me. But Andrew has heard them talkin' amongst themselves. Still, 'tis only John who's been addressed directly. Andrew and I appear to be noticed nae at all when we're among them."

Now, in full wonderment, I pressed further, "And you believe that this is true, and that you have not been deceived by your own imaginings?"

Now came a definite flash of anger in the dark eyes and she slammed her hand upon the table, "And d'ye think I could be the teacher of the bairnies in this village were I given to crazy imaginings or the purveying o' falsehoods?"

Seeing her distress at my doubts, I apologized and tried to shift the conversation to more neutral pleasantries. In this manner of general talk, we passed perhaps half an hour's time before a tall young gentleman entered the room.

Sara called out to him, "John, 'tis the traveler who spoke with Andrew upon the cliffs this very mornin'. Come and join us."

The man, rugged of face and possessed of huge arms and powerful looking hands, came over to the table. Whereupon I stood and offered my hand, which he took, and smiled in a most friendly manner.

"Eyup. I am John, the blacksmith o' this fine town. And who would you be?"

I said, "Just a traveler. I have no profession. I *was* a man of science—a doctor—but I have lately taken to traveling in search of meanings that science could not supply."

"Then 'tis a worthy, if impossible, journey you pursue."

"Why impossible?" I asked, startled by his directness.

"Because you seek the truth, and the truth cannot be known."

I let this remark foment for a minute. I thought about how I struggled to understand the meaning of the death of all that I loved, and I wondered again what I really hoped to learn in my travels.

John interrupted the uncertainties now cascading in my mind, "And what does your truth-seeking tell you concerning the veracity of the experience that Andrew and Sara have surely told you of by now?"

I hesitated, weighing my words before I answered, "In truth, I seek not to judge, but only to record those things that come to me as being in the realm of the inexplicable; experienced nevertheless by myself, or shared by several independent and separate souls."

"Well, add this to your awareness then that I, too, have stood on the cliffs, taking my place among the knights. But for me, one thing is different. I can see them, and they see me. Indeed, they have spoken to me."

"What have they said?" I was listening eagerly.

"They ask if the people still remember. And do we trust that the knights stand guard, even today?"

"How do you answer?" I could barely contain my excitement, looking from Sara's face to John's and back.

John, his eyes trained on my face, spoke softly, even reverently, "I tell them that some scoff and some trust. I tell them that I trust because I see the truth of their presence. It seemed to me that they were well pleased with this, as King Arthur himself, resplendent in his long robe and crown, then rode to where I stood and touched me with his sword upon my shoulder."

Now I wondered what should I make of all this. It was a verified experience, true, but so fanciful that doubts swarmed my mind like flies. I knew the next question was more than a little insulting, and still, I had to ask it, if only to judge his response, "How can I know that you have not simply fired each other's imaginations with this tale and expanded on it, each for the other?"

John, his face composed and showing none of the anger I'd feared I might provoke, answered without hesitation, "I cannot tell you how you can obtain inner certainty. Is na' that the purpose of your travel? Perhaps you will go again upon the cliffs, and perhaps another time, see them yourself."

In that moment, I resolved to do just that.

I stayed in the village for two weeks more, but though I walked each day along the cliffs, I saw nothing of the knights. Yet, on my last day, as I was about to leave the cliff's edge, I would swear that I heard the pounding of horses' hooves, and under my feet the ground vibrated as if with heavy steeds, racing the wind across the high moorland, to turn back whatever enemies might come.

And although some of my doubts remained, I decided to record these tales, so surely and convincingly told, by an old man, a teacher, and a blacksmith.

Fig. 4: Drawing of Knight.

Fig. 5: Statue of King Arthur

~IV~
Kinsale, Ireland – May 9th, 1888

I left Cornwall on a stormy afternoon and took the unpleasant journey by ship from Fishgard in Wales to Roslaire, Ireland. I was aware that some members of my family had sailed from Ireland a century before, from the harbor at Cork, and I determined that that would be a good place to do some research into their circumstances.

I traveled by rail from Roslaire to Cork, and once there, went directly to the customs house to seek records of ships and passages. The records held there were extensive, and I found them so well catalogued that it was a straightforward, if tedious, task to locate the surname of Trevy, which I knew as the line of my father's great-grandfather's family.

Within these lists I found that a certain Aldus Trevy had departed Ireland in the year 1791, and traveled to Philadelphia, Pennsylvania, which city I knew to be the original port of entry for the Trevy line. I discovered that he had sailed, not from Cork as was the family legend, but from Kinsale, a few miles south of Cork, and that he made his journey in second class aboard the ship *Printemps*.

Upon further inquiry, I was surprised to discover that the *Printemps* was, by odd coincidence, maintained in Kinsale as a museum ship. With that knowledge, my next step was determined, and I took the next train to Kinsale.

The harbor town of Kinsale was at once bustling and quaint. Narrow streets wound up and down a steep hill to the quay. Many sailing ships lay at anchor in the harbor and several more at the dock, engaged in off-loading or on-loading. It was clear where the active dockside lay, but as the harbor was long and well-sheltered, a second quayside development lay to the northwest. There, I was told, was berthed the *Printemps*, permanently maintained along the wharf and open for informational tours on Wednesdays and Fridays. As my arrival was on a Tuesday, my next order of business was to secure lodging.

Calling in at the James Edwards Tavern, I found rooms, the modest fee for which included a very generous dinner offering. The weather having continued stormy in the days following my passage from Fishgard, I retired to my room and spent the afternoon recording some notes regarding my travels. I was not inclined to record the particulars of local sights as might the typical traveler, rather, I felt the requirement to note my more unexpected encounters, in the hope of finding in them some hidden meaning beyond their fascination as peculiar occurrences.

What, I wondered, could be the larger meaning of such legends and reports of things not readily explained? I had been set upon this task beginning with my own encounter with the Farquhar Clan, which came and went in my memory like a dream or hallucination, altering the impressions of my senses and challenging the reliability of my experience. I would have written the whole night off in the manner of the barkeep—as a delusion generated by too much drink—but for the extreme clarity of the events, the precise recall of details which is not typical of dreams or delirium, and foremost, putting physical challenge squarely in opposition to all mental doubt, the very real dagger which lay upon my writing desk.

I sought also to record that point of understanding concerning the experience—granted, not my own, but one consistently and vividly reported—regarding the appearance of the knights of King Arthur upon the high cliffs. As told to me, this was more than legend; it was a solid experience of physical reality according to the people who reported it to me, supported as well by the historical record of the good friars, written at the time of the occurrence.

In both cases, I felt there was a common core, but I had yet to fully discover it, let alone articulate it in a precise manner. What were the aspects that brought these so vividly dissimilar stories together to create the sense I had of their shared meaning? I decided to make a list of possibilities—candidates, if you will—for explanation. Thus I recorded it that rainy afternoon.

1. *All three tales have persons from a former time appearing long after they would usually be considered too old or certainly deceased.*
2. *In all tales, the figures appear in flesh and blood with objects in tangible and physical forms.*
3. *The people were heroic figures from an historical past.*
4. *All occurrences gave rise to either belief or scorn among locals of the area.*
5. *In each story, life appeared to extend beyond its natural time, extending its reach into the present from a distant past.*

On the other hand, there were distinct differences between the three, and perceiving these, I realized that I would need to record them as well.

1. *Two events were personally relevant to me, while the other was not.*
2. *I was both observer and participant in two, while in the other, it was others who experienced the occurrence and I did not.*

3. *One had been recorded in the annals of history, and related to grand historical events; one was local and current, while the last was singular; built upon the nexus of ancient past and living present.*
   4. *Two were verified by multiple observers reporting independently that which they saw, while the veracity of the other was largely based on my own testimony.*
   5. *One had brought an actual enduring object—the dagger—to bear witness, while no physical evidence of the others remained.*

Though I sought to find one principle in these facts that could give them an overarching meaning, I could not articulate any such notion. I decided that I would need, therefore, to continue on my journey and let fate and circumstance add to my experience and insight.

My sleep this night was visited with dream images of Spanish ships, of knights, horses, and clansmen, but when I awoke, I could recall them all as nothing more than that: dream images, wrapped in their mantles of otherworld reality, which are shed within seconds of waking.

The weather having turned to the better, I rose to full daylight streaming through my window. I dressed hurriedly and went down to breakfast in the lower hall of the inn. The room was largely empty at this hour, most guests having breakfasted earlier and gone off on their way. I nevertheless chose to ask if I might join one of the other guests who remained, a gentleman whose dress suggested that he, too, was traveling. He greeted me in a friendly manner and I sat.

No sooner had I settled into my chair, than the gentleman began to quiz me regarding the reason for my visit to Kinsale, but as his questions seemed to bear no suspicion, only genuine open curiosity, I told him of my interest in tracing my family and specifically learning more about one Aldus Trevy who had sailed from this port nearly one hundred years ago.

"What," he inquired, "would ye think to find of value in knowing about this distant relative." For the moment, I was at a loss as to what to say. I had taken it as a given that it was worthwhile to learn about one's family and one's past. Still, I knew not what specifically to name as that value, so I admitted to him that I was, myself, not yet clear what might be the gain in such pursuits.

"'Tis a fool's errand," he informed me, but then apologized for being too frank. I urged him to elaborate his view, and he continued thus, "The past is dead and the dead are dead. Living is of the present and of those still living. What profit can there be in learning about persons or things which can neither be altered, nor able to advance now any contribution beyond what is already done, and already part of our modern knowledge?"

What he said seemed indisputably true, and yet I found that in my heart, I was uneasy with such a view.

Somehow, for me, it was the truth of my recent past, coupled with the loss of my parents and wife, that made connection to my roots seem more necessary; more vital. But lacking a way to articulate this, I simply smiled, assenting that there did seem to be little tangible benefit in my quest.

Taking my leave, I thanked the innkeeper for a fine and satisfying breakfast and headed down to the *Printemps* for a tour of this aged ship that just may have been the very vessel my distant kin sailed upon to America.

A small group had gathered with me in the interest of seeing the vessel, and in the few minutes we stood there waiting, I listened to hear if any were talking about seeking knowledge of kin who had sailed aboard the *Printemps,* or perhaps just sailed from this port. But all that I heard seemed to be the common chitty-chat about the weather, about the poor conditions in the guest houses, and other such complaints.

As I stood there awaiting our guide, whose arrival was promised promptly at ten o'clock, I withdrew a few steps from the group and was leaning over the rail, amused by the small fish being pursued by gulls below. My reverie was broken by the croaky voice of a woman calling harshly, "Come along!" Looking up, I discovered that the others had already mounted the gang plank and were waiting on the *Printemps'* deck.

The old woman continued to scold me as I hurried to catch up, "Dinna be lagging, lad, for I have news for ye, if ye care t'listen," and feeling chagrined, I followed at the rear of the group as we were led below, down into the ship. Our guide took us through the various areas of the ship, from first and second class berths to Captain's quarters, to the galley, and even into the cargo hold and steerage areas. Especially the last of these areas were oppressively cramped, and I grew claustrophobic at the thought of weeks spent in such dank, dark and constrained space.

When she returned to the second class passenger area, our guide sat down upon a bench and bade us to also take seats on other benches arranged across from her.

Her "news" as she had called it began thus, "This ship made, all told, thirty-six voyages from this port to various ports in America, and returned. For the most part, 'twas passengers leaving Ireland that filled the ship outbound, and varied cargo that filled her holds on the trips back, as few were choosing to return to Ireland. Now that accounts for six thousand souls or more that made their way across the ocean.

"Of course some fell short, falling sick t'be buried at sea, especially those who were particularly poor and crossing in steerage. Others, wealthy passengers, might've enjoyed the three-month-long journey . . . when not caught in storms.

"Second class travelers were not as fortunate as the three or four family groups who took their ease in first class, but they at least had adequate food for the journey and were generally able to keep warm and dry.

"The *Printemps* was considered a good luck ship since she made so many successful crossings with no such disastrous difficulties as befell many less fortunate ships in the rough waters of the North Atlantic. Now, let me tell ye a few tales of particular travelers . . . and well I remember these stories."

The old woman told of the Randalls who traveled with such excessive wealth that even their maid and butler slept in first class berths. She told of the Burrills who, though they were traveling in first class, lost a small daughter to fever during the voyage, and of her mother who was so overcome with sorrow that she threw herself overboard and could not be recovered. The mother in this sad tale was, the old woman said, most especially beautiful, and wore her most beautiful green gown and all of her jewelry, a great ruby ring, and a sapphire and diamond necklace, as well as diamond earrings, shaped, ironically, like falling tear drops.

The old woman also said that the daughter who died mirrored her mother's looks to an uncanny degree, having the same fine nose and sweet lips, and that as the child's body, wrapped in its winding cloth, was slipped off the rail to be buried at sea, the mother cried into the wind, "I'll not leave ye long alone, my darling!"

That very night, escaping the watchful eyes of her family, she leapt into the foam. At the telling, a brief sob escaped the old woman and then, blowing her nose with a large, brightly colored kerchief, she continued, "Among the passengers in second class, there were so many stories of triumph . . . and tragedy."

Sweeping her arm in an arc from one end of the second class berths to the other, she told of the woman who, at each meal, broke her own bread and gave half to a child down in steerage. The old woman's eyes became moist and she brought out her kerchief once more as she pronounced, "Such heroism. Such humanity."

My breath quickened as her stories went on, "Let me tell ye now of the doctor who traveled on this ship, leaving Ireland for a new life in America. On this ship, miracles were accomplished by his gifted hands. Children were brought into this world who, what with twisted cords and bleeding, would not have survived had it not been for him. Mothers were saved. Not one mother but two, and several severe lacerations amongst the sailors were sewn and treated, likely saving them from the bone-cutter's saw, for the men, ye see, preferred Dr. Trevy to the ship's own surgeon."

As she pronounced the doctor's name, my heart gave a jolt, and I let out a short, involuntary cry of astonishment.

"So ye know the name of Dr. Trevy, do ye, boyo? And 'tis no surprise to me who recognized ye from the first." The old woman's words struck my ears clearly enough, but I could make no sense of them.

As I sat dumb before her, she stood and addressed me sharply. "Are ye not the man who seeks his lineage in tracing back to the Trevy family and dear, dear Dr. Trevy?" Her tone was nearly a rebuke, which I did not understand, but I managed to stammer, "Yes. Yes, I am that man. But why do you call me out in connection to this very man, Dr. Trevy?"

"As to how, I have no answer, but as to the fact, I have no doubt. I did recognize ye and see in yourself the same good and kindness and life-giving gifts as Dr. Trevy. And ye share his profession, do ye not?"

By now, the other members of our group were staring, first at the old woman and then at me, wonderment written upon their faces.

"It is true that I am a doctor and it is true that my kin by the name of Trevy, traveled on this ship . . . as far as I have been able to determine. I came here seeking some further particulars and verification of these facts."

The woman then smiled at me and said "So now ye have it, Doctor. Verification, and the truth as best I can remember it."

Fig. 6 The ship Printemps

~V~
On the way to Svalta, Poland – June 7th, 1888

It was while staying in Kinsale that I met Vanya, the Russian. Once again, it was the local pub that provided the place of meeting. I was sitting alone, as often was the case, taking a long time with my beer, when Vanya entered. Wearing a riding cloak, his hair cut extremely short in military fashion, and with a sword in the belted scabbard around his waist, he seemed a figure out of place and time.

Dusty boots pounded the wooden planks as he crossed the floor in long strides, then, speaking harshly in a language I did not recognize as any Western European tongue, he demanded a drink of the barman . . . or so I suspected.

When the barman did little more than stare at him with a puzzled expression, the Russian threw himself across the bar, grabbed a bottle of vodka, snorted, and turning with a flourish, his cape swirling out behind, marched directly to my table and plopped down. The poor barman was frozen in place, open-mouthed, hands raised, as though he expected to be shot at any moment.

Vanya let out a deep-throated laugh and, to my great surprise, said in good, though heavily-accented, English, "I have frightened him, do you think? No?" And then he laughed again. "Have no fear, my friend. I have come to join you!"

By now, I was growing used to people presenting themselves to me out of the blue, and getting to be a bit less surprised when someone sat down uninvited at whichever table I happened to occupy, so I said simply, "You are welcome at my table."

"NO!" he roared, "Not join you at your table. I mean, join you in your journey!"

At that, I was dumbfounded. I knew this man not at all and could not fathom how he knew of me, let alone my travels.

As though answering my thought, he said, "I have been following you. I followed from Scotland to England and now to Ireland. I had to know what it was that you were seeking, and now, I believe I do. So I will join you, for I, too, am a seeker."

"And what is it that you think I seek?"

"Life! Life triumphing over death. It is what a soldier seeks in every battle. It is at the heart of heroism, because even the fallen warrior achieves his immortality if he will but fight bravely and overcome his fear."

"But I am no soldier!" I objected.

"No matter," he waved dismissively, "You are on a march. You are on a campaign. I will join you. I will pledge my allegiance to you!" he shouted, frightening the barman again, and before I could blink, he grabbed my hand and shook it thoroughly.

"I am Captain Shemtzgravia," he announced, "Captain *Vanya* Shemtzgravia. You will call me Vanya."

"Do I have a choice in this matter?" I queried weakly.

"No! None at all. I am meant to share your journey. Now, we must hurry away from here. You have much to see, much to learn."

"Hurry whence? I have made no plan."

"To Poland. To the village of Svalta. It is nearly time for the celebration."

And so unsure was I at that time as to what I was to do, and certainly overwhelmed by Captain Shemtzgravia—*Vanya*—finding in him such force, such sincerity, and such conviction, that I resolved without further question to accept his companionship.

The very next day, we were on the dock in Kinsale, boarding the ship that would take us to Bremerhaven, Germany, from which port we would travel overland to Poland.

The journey this time, again through rough seas, took twenty days. As soon as we landed, I, being thoroughly worn out from the storm-tossed crossing, Vanya insisted that we hire a coach and travel at full speed to

Svalta. "The festival is in less than a month. We must travel day and night."

After a mad ride, pressing on through days and nights, we arrived in the village of Svalta, Poland just before dawn on the 7th of June, 1888. Vanya directed our driver to the home of Mrs. Drvorska, and as soon as the coach had drawn up at the front door, he leapt out and dashed to the front door. It was a small house, and as he approached it, the door flew open, exposing a round, flat-faced woman with an enormous bosom, arms opened wide, calling "Captain! Captain! You have returned again!"

Vanya swept this lady into his arms and made to lift her off her feet, but quickly settled for merely stretching her up, then settling her down once more, as her bulk prevented her from actually leaving the ground. Kisses on both checks were exchanged and then Vanya spoke, "But I could not fail to come. And look . . . " he waved for me to approach, "I have brought a true friend."

"Come in, come in!" Mrs. Drvorska opened her arms and drew me in, fairly engulfing me, and exclaimed in passably good English, "Blessings, blessings and welcome to our Christinafest. But come in, eat first, and then we will go to the village square."

Over a hearty breakfast, I asked Vanya if Christinafest was a church holiday, as it was not one that I was aware of. He shook his head and told me that this was not Christ the Savior who was being celebrated, rather, it was the girl, Christina, who had " . . . brought life to the village when death had come to gather her."

I started to ask more, but Vanya stood up abruptly and told me, "You will know by seeing and by dancing and by singing. You will come. Now."

We went by foot, for it was but a short distance to the village square, and there on the cobbled court, surrounded by shops and stalls, the villagers were gathering. All were dressed in what appeared to be their finest clothes; ladies in dresses with full skirts in marvelous reds and blues with starched white aprons, their hair done up in braids and flowers and garlands; the men in knickerbocker breeches and high black boots, with white billowing shirts which were set off by vests that sparkled with shiny stones, sequins and beads.

Everyone was greeting everyone, embracing and laughing. Pigs and children ran between people's legs, and sheep trotted here and there through the throng. Such joy arose from this assemblage that I found my own self laughing and even leaping; not feeling like a stranger, but cuffing people on the back and ruffling the children's hair as I moved among the crowd.

Before long, a band of musicians came together in the midst of the throng and the joyful sounds of dance music began to entice the crowd into circles and pairs as the celebration began in earnest. Dancing swirled into drinking and games, and then more dancing. A feast, highlighted by several great roast boars, was brought out and all were invited to partake. It was all conducted without formality; people grabbing meat and bread, or spooning out great helpings of potatoes and squash from many hot, black cauldrons to heap upon their plates.

The afternoon rolled on with more dancing and drinking, and then, upon a signal from the band, a man, perhaps a bit more richly decked out than the rest, stood upon a rough platform and made an announcement. I did not understand his words, but as soon as he stepped down, the band began to play a most beautiful, lilting march, and from the four corners of the square, lines of children—tiny ones to nearly grown—all marched into the center, strewing flowers from their baskets.

From out of their midst appeared a thin and lovely young girl of about ten, dressed in perfect white, her hair braided in elaborate flower-laced plaits, who came to a stop in the center and then began to dance, while all the people standing 'round about her clapped and clapped in time. Faster and faster she spun, until I myself became dizzy. On and on she turned, whirling and twirling, for ten minutes and longer, until suddenly, she fell to the ground, unconscious.

I started forward, but hands gripped my arms, preventing me from interference.

As I watched, the women came forward and lifted the girl gently onto a flower-bedecked litter, and with the music now somber, they carried her slowly, 'round and around. This continued for three or four long minutes during which time the entire crowd seemed to be holding its collective breath.

I, too, found myself seized with a disturbing mix of emotions; such lingering joy from the dancing and feasting and such sorrow to see this poor child lying still and unconscious.

And then, the little one in white sat up. She smiled brilliantly, and waved to the crowd which burst out into the most jubilant sound I have ever heard; a great mixture of voices singing and shouting; bells ringing, and hands clapping. At once the square was again a whirl of dancing and laughter as the little girl jumped down from her stretcher and ran from one person to the next, accepting hugs and kisses and twirling with each person after person, in happy celebration.

The merrymaking ran on into the night until the darkness was complete. Then, bearing candles, the villagers began to disperse, walking slowly back to their homes.

I saw Vanya coming toward me, he having disappeared early and myself having spent the day alone . . . but not really alone for even a moment. Behind him came Mrs. Drvorska, and each was carrying a small lamp. Vanya handed me his lamp, and tossing his arm around my shoulder in the way of an old friend, said, "Come. We will go home now," and back we strolled through the now quiet town to Mrs. Drvorska's house.

Though I was filled with wonder and questions, I was so tired that I went immediately to bed and instantly to sleep, not waking until the sun was well up. When I came down, Vanya and Mrs. Drvorska were waiting at the table for me.

"Well, what did you make of our Christina Celebration?" asked Vanya, sipping rich, thick coffee.

"It was . . . rather remarkable," I started weakly, realizing even as I said it that my words did little justice to the event, "Yes . . . ah, fantastic. Ah . . . joyful . . . beyond measure," I stammered in incomplete phrases.

"Yes, but did you gather the meaning?" Vanya's eager expression encouraged me to answer and I struggled to gather my thoughts.

"It seemed to celebrate life and youth, but then, when the poor girl exhausted herself, it was as though she died and was being . . . born away. Then, like a resurrection, she came back to herself . . . to us; life-filled and healthy, and everyone celebrated with love and joy once more."

"Good. Yes, is good. You have seen and you have understood, so now you will sit and I will tell you the story behind the celebration." Vanya motioned to an empty chair and I sat gratefully, accepting hot coffee and a tender smile from Mrs. Drvorska.

"Many, many years ago—more than three hundred and fifty years ago—in this very village, a plague came and many people died. There was, naturally, great sorrow and despair.

"One little girl, Christina, seemed untouched by the hopelessness. She danced and played and gathered flowers to take to the sick, and everyone believed that she was so good and so kind and so gentle, that death would not touch her. But then, she, too, became sick.

"In just a few days, it appeared that Christina would die. She lay upon her bed as her mother bathed her head with cool water . . . and tears.

"The village prepared for yet another funeral, and hopelessness grew deeper until it reached the deepest places in the hearts of the villagers." Vanya reached over to pat Mrs. Dvorskza's hand before continuing, "But on the morrow, when everyone expected to hear the news that the precious child had died, her mother burst out of her house and shouted, 'She lives! She has come up out of her bed and is well!'

"Word spread instantly and everyone who was able came to the square to learn more of this miracle. They were rewarded by the sight of Christina, coming out of her house, her face shining and pink, her hair in beautiful braids interlaced with flowers, and wearing her best dress of purest white.

"Then Christina began to dance and twirl, and she bade everyone join her, and for that whole day, the village feasted and danced, celebrating that death had passed the little girl over."

Fig. 7: Christinafest Celebration

Vanya continued, "By night, all the villagers returned to their homes in high spirits, feeling that now, perhaps, the worst was over. But in the morning, as the people began their day, those crossing the square heard the weeping from inside Christina's house.

"The little girl had gone to bed, full of life and joy, but sometime during the night, death had returned.

"It seemed doubly cruel. What could the meaning be? Why did Christina come back, rise out of her death bed to dance and sing and give them all hope, only to be swallowed up once more by the dark. What cruel God had done this thing?

"No one spoke of Christina and her day of recovery, except perhaps in whispers behind hands. A year passed and the sickness continued. More people died and almost every day, someone new became ill. So many days were marked by death.

"It is possible—even probable—that no one noticed on that first anniversary of Christina's recovery, or perhaps on the second anniversary, or even the third. But by the fourth year after she had come back to life, talk among the villagers began to acknowledge that on this day, for each of the last four years, no one had become sick. No one had died.

"By the fifth anniversary of Christina's death, the pattern was undeniable. No sickness came on the anniversary day, and no death either.

"Indeed, for that one day, the sick even seemed better; they brightened, and the village began first, to be thankful and then, to realize that Christina had somehow brought them a small but wonderful gift; that for one day each year, there was, in Svalta, no sickness. No death.

"Year after year, it continued. As death and sickness passed over without stopping on each anniversary of Christina's Day of Joy, the people began to understand, and then to celebrate; for they knew that while there was no escape from mortality, on that one day, for us here in Svalta, Christina's gift brought life; continuous and joyful. The lives of our children became even more precious, and the laughter and embraces of both young and old alike engendered in us such joy as to overpower the suffering and sadness of illnesses—even plague—that we had faced yesterday and would face again tomorrow.

"Christina's day became a day of celebration; a celebration that continues to this day." Raising his hands in a manner of supplication, Vanya added the final and most telling part of the miracle, "And on this day, for over 350 years now, there is nothing but life in Svalta.

"And that, my friend, is why I brought you here. It is another part of your lessons on this journey. And you are not finished yet!"

Vanya reached into a basket brimming with Mrs. Dvorska's fragrant muffins and stuffed one whole into his mouth.

"We must travel on!" he said, chewing enthusiastically, "Tomorrow, we leave!"

"And where will we go?" I asked, not sure if I should be excited or dismayed by the prospect.

"To Norway. To the land of the Vikings, for they, too, have a story for you."

~VI~
Vanya's Own Story

It had been the rule on our travels for Vanya to take his own room or, more often when it was possible, he chose to sleep in the barn with the horses. This, he explained, was how an officer of the cavalry should spend his night.

So it was on one occasion, as we reached the only *gasthouse* on a long and lonely road, that Vanya inspected the rude enclosure which passed for its stable and concluded that the space was barely large enough for the horse, thus affording no space where he might sleep. This, and the dreadful stench of the pigs the owner of the establishment kept in the stalls alongside the horses, meant that Vanya, to his disgust, must pass the night in the inn.

But so small was this particular *gasthouse* that there were only two rooms for hire, and as the one room was already occupied by five men, traveling together, there was no choice but to take the room remaining. We hoped quite fervently that no other travelers would come along later, since we were certain the proprietor would have happily collected his coin and trundled them in to join us, there being still room enough on the floor for a few pallets.

After a dinner, if you could call it that, of astonishingly tasteless goulash soup and black bread, Vanya and I retired, finding in our room, one bed, two straight wooden chairs, and a small table upon which we placed a bottle of red wine brought along for the trip and much needed this night, with two tin goblets borrowed from the kitchen.

We sat at our table, sharing the wine, and soon discovered that the airless space under the gable that was our room, was stifling hot. It was at this point that Vanya stood, and without apology or excuse, took off his jacket and shirt. His body was well-muscled and strong, and I felt a bit self-conscious at the idea of my stripping down also. Still, the room was like a furnace, so I removed my jacket, but only rolled up my shirtsleeves. I found it awkward, not knowing where to look, as Vanya sat across from me, even after my years as a physician.

No doubt noting my discomfort, Vanya roared with laughter and remarked, "Is not such a pleasant sight, is it?" I frowned, not really understanding until Vanya stood and pointed to a great scar on his belly which I had not seen up until this point.

"There is a story behind this old wound," he informed me, and turning his back, exposed an even more dreadful scar half-way up. "The wound is here also," he said, turning to face me again as I gasped, realizing that he must have been run through with a sword or saber. And picturing the array of internal organs which would have been at risk with such an injury . . . my mind could not hold the fact of his survival.

Sensing my discomfort, Vanya hesitated, "Shall I tell you? It *is*, I think, the reason I am here to travel with you."

I nodded my assent, and Vanya, reversing his chair and stretching forward across the back of it, poured himself a glass of wine before filling my cup as well.

"We were fighting in Prussia," he began. "There were constant raids between our countries. I was, as you know, with the Russian Cavalry. We had come down to a small village which we believed to be largely unprotected, there to raid supplies, but a sizable force of Prussians who had hidden themselves in the barns surprised us.

"A tremendous battle rose up, and my men and I found that we were badly outnumbered. There was no choice but to try to fight our way out, but we were surrounded. By afternoon, most of my men had fallen, and in a last hopeless effort, five of my fellows and I formed a line and rushed at the enemy in a death-defying charge, hoping for a miracle that would allow us to break through.

"But the enemy held and I was pulled from my horse. Hand-to-hand fighting followed, and as I engaged three soldiers in front of me, I suddenly felt a searing pain in my back, and then, looking down, I saw the point of the sword that had pierced me through. I fell to my knees and somehow managed to turn, firing the ball from my last pistol and blowing a hole in the head of the man who had struck me, before falling to the ground with his sword still piercing my body. I knew all was lost and that I would soon die."

Vanya sipped his wine and gathered his thoughts before going on.

"As I lay there, all became quiet, and as the blood seeped from my wounds, my head became cloudy, and all went dark.

"Sometime later, I awoke to the voices of soldiers walking among us, speaking in German. I knew little of the language, but the word *tod* . . . I knew that to mean *dead*. I heard gunshots and muffled cries behind me, and I understood that the enemy soldiers were dispatching any of my comrades who they determined were not already dead." Vanya's hand trembled ever so slightly and the emotion in his voice was clear.

"Anxiety seized my heart, even though I knew that I would certainly die from my wound. Still, the ignominy of being shot while lying there drawing my last breath made me afraid, and then angry. I imagined myself gathering one last burst of strength to turn and confront the enemy, but it was at that very moment, I heard the voice of my comrade, Tasch. His voice was very low, but his words were distinct, 'Rest quiet,' he told me, 'We are dead.'

"I was about to protest, to tell him, 'No, I'm still here,' when I realized that he was telling me to feign death so that the Germans would pass us by. I lay there, holding my breath, and indeed, the soldiers walked by laughing, repeating, 'Tod, tod, tod.'

"I lay there, quiet for what seemed to me to be a very long time before I felt the sword being drawn from my body and something being stuffed under my tunic, and heard, 'Get up.'

"It was Tasch, urging me to rise. I thought it impossible, but he hooked his hand under my shoulder and struggled to lift me up. I rose, first to my knees and then to my feet, and then stood swaying as Tasch stuffed more cloths against my wounds to staunch the blood which the sword, sheathed within my body, had held back. Then he wrapped my arm around his neck, fitted his shoulder into my armpit, and began to move me forward, almost carrying me.

"We moved in this manner to some nearby woods where all was silent. For just a moment we rested and then Tasch urged me on and further on until we came to a clearing and a farm house. I squeezed my eyes shut once, then twice as I looked at the farm, the house, the barn, because they looked familiar to me; like a scene from my childhood, though I had not been on this side of the wood before that day. Not ever, that I knew.

"Stumbling, being dragged along by Tasch, we reached the door of the farm house and Tasch knocked. A woman appeared almost at once, and when I looked in her face, I cried out, 'Mama!' and all went black once more.

"Some time later, I returned to my senses and found myself lying on a bed. Someone was bathing my head with cool water and my chest was wrapped tightly with clean white cloth. I stared up into the woman's face, and said again, 'Mama.'

"And this time, she answered me! 'Quiet, Vanya. You must be quiet and lie still,' she said to me.

"So I rested back, but turned my head to watch her as she moved about the room. My mind could make no sense of how she could be there. She seemed to be my own mother, but my mother had died years ago. I had watched her as she lay dying, her pretty face ruined with sores from the pox, her breathing jagged, until at last, she drew breath no more. But now, she was here, and her face was lovely again.

"The room was but dimly lit and it took a few minutes before I realized that there was a young boy standing at the foot of the bed, a candle in his hand. By that light I could see him clearly. It was my brother, Peter. My little brother, who had—years before—fallen from his horse and hit his head upon a rock. My little brother, who had died instantly.

"What madness is this? I wondered. Am I delirious? I called out for Tasch, but the woman—my mother?—said he had gone, and that I would not see him again, not for a long time.

"Then, turning to a girl standing behind her she said, 'Tatiana, I need fresh water.' Silently the girl turned and went out, carrying the pitcher from the table beside the bed with her. But there was something about the way she moved, something about her blond hair that seemed so familiar to me. I struggled to focus my thoughts.

"And when the girl returned with the water, I saw that she was my sister, Tatiana, and I spoke to her.

"'Tatie, is it you?' I asked, and in a voice so familiar it almost made me weep, she answered, 'Yes, Vanya. We are all here. We will take care of you and you will live. That is why we are here.'

"Where is Victor?" I asked, hungry for news of my other brother.

"'He is in St. Petersburg with Father. He is a priest. He cares for our Father while you ride with the army. He lives, and so cannot be here. So it is also for our Father, who is also still alive,' she chattered on happily, 'but you will see them both one day soon when your travels take you back home. For now, just lie back and try to sleep.'

"When I awoke, hours or perhaps days later, the bandage was gone from my body and I was astounded to see my wound completely healed. An ugly, red-welted scar remained where the sword had pierced, but there was now little pain. I swung my feet to the floor and found that I could stand. It seemed impossible.

"No one else was in the room, but on the table, sat a bowl of soup and a freshly baked loaf of bread. I was ravishingly hungry, so I devoured it all. Then I went to the door and called out, 'Mama? Peter? Tatie?' But there was no answer. I returned to the bed where, neatly arrayed, were my boots, a clean shirt, and my tunic—now repaired.

"After I dressed, I went into the dooryard and called, again and again, but there was no answer. I searched the barn and there found my horse, my saddle already in place. I mounted and rode out to search the farm for my family; all those persons I knew to be deceased, each and every one, but who had somehow tended and healed me, but they were nowhere.

"At last I dismounted and, putting my head against a tree, I wept, calling their names quietly to myself, for I knew in my heart that they could not return.

"Then I remounted and rode away, back to Russia, traveling many days. I returned to Saint Petersburg and found my brother in his priest's robes caring for my Father, just as I had been told.

"I told them how I had seen my mother, my brother, and my sister. I told them how I had been healed. But they just shook their heads.

"I asked about my friend Tasch, if they had heard of his return. 'Dead,' my father said, 'Found dead, lying where he fell.'

"After only one day's time in the city, I could remain no longer. I did not rejoin my regiment, but instead struck off on the long wandering path that has led me to you. I have since heard that I was declared lost in battle; thought to have died."

Vanya stretched, smiling broadly, his eyes twinkling with humor, "But I am here. Here with you, my traveler friend, and we are akin in discovering and knowing what few know."

And with those words, he raised his glass and made this toast, 'To life . . . and death . . . and all their mysteries.'"

~VII~
Lenvaartkii, Norway – July 4th, 1888

We abandoned our coach in Stockholm, Sweden at Vanya's urging, because he insisted that from there, the roads would be unfit for travel by any means other than horseback. For the first day out of Stockholm, I cursed Vanya; his insistence, his presence, and especially, his love of horses. But by the third day, I had become both more comfortable in the saddle, and more accepting of the fact that the trails we traveled were little more than tracks and clearly impassable by any other means. On horseback, we could make a good distance each day, and we stopped each evening at the first reasonable house or way-station that presented itself. We had no hard deadline as before with Svalta. Still, as the summer season in this region was brief—and an early winter would surely block our return—we chose not to delay.

The landscape was rugged, and unlike anything I had seen before, vast and open, and as we came into the seaside region of Stavanger, the beauty of the place settled deeply into my soul.

The small village of Lenvaartkii lay on a sea inlet, surrounded by steep cliffs. Small boats were drawn up on the shingle at the water's edge; a pale, yet beautiful reminder of the bold Viking past of this area. Vanya, who knew the workings of this village, took me to find the chief; the people hereabouts being still organized in tribal fashion, stemming from the days of the warriors. We quickly reached the home of Thodrajvgga, the village leader, who had no first name and thus was addressed only by his family name. We were quickly invited in, and passed under the low lintel in a crouch. The house was rude but comfortable, with benches all around the edge of a great room that was at once kitchen, dining, and living room for Thodrajvgga and his family. We had arrived at sunset and they were just gathering for supper. Our hosts bid Vanya and I join them.

After we ate—a delicious chowder with fish, potatoes and onion followed by rich, cheese-filled pastries—the children went off up a ladder to the loft, and Thodrajvgga's wife retired to their bedroom behind a curtain.

Left to our own, three men, smoking, and drinking a hot beverage of uncertain ingredients and a bitter taste, Vanya told Thodrajvgga of my journey, and in particular, about my interest in the inexplicable.

Thodrajvgga gave me a broad smile and began to speak in his language. Vanya, after some moments, held up his hand and, addressing Thodrajvgga, also in his language and I in mine, explained that he would translate, in order that I might understand the tale. In this manner, Thodrajvgga speaking, then pausing while Vanya translated, and with much waving of arms and even role play or charade for the sword fighting, the tale was told.

"Back in the good days, the days of mist and clouds and the rule of the gods, the men of this village were renowned for their bold raids and their valor in battle. In our harsh land of Norway, there was little chance to live by farming, and little opportunity for trade. The manner of our existence was through the commerce of raiding. To this purpose, the great Viking ships were built, and the tradition of invasion and marauding became the center of our Norse culture and existence. It was a matter of survival and a standard of heroic living. The purpose of a man's life was to secure life for his village and his family, to live bravely, and to die bravely; thus to enter the halls of heroes and gods that was Valhalla.

"Many great chiefs had led the men of this village on raids across the seas to Scotland, to Ireland, and to Iceland. Some even claimed to have sailed to unknown lands far beyond Iceland, but such is the bragging and mythology of men returning from voyages, and not all tales are to be believed.

"But on one story, all were agreed. First, because it told of near defeat, and second, because it was told by so many, without variation." Thodrajvgga looked at me sternly and shook his finger as Vanya translated this last, "A tale of near defeat, you understand . . . this was a thing that no Viking would tell if it were not absolutely true, and then, with great reluctance.

"And so it was that on a certain raid to the Irish shore, the men of Lenvaartkii came against a force of men who were waiting for them, armed to the extreme and determined to defend what was theirs to the last man. Our men were led on that voyage by Ddvadajk, a great and victorious hero.

"But on this foray, in spite of his great skill and bravery, when his men were surrounded by the enemy, Ddvadajk was himself struck down, and lay on the ground, gravely wounded while his men fought and fell around him.

"In the village, the Chief's son, Dnard, who had seen thirteen winters and had begged to accompany his father on the raid—which suit had been denied—fell to the ground as he practiced his sword work, crying out, 'My father is undone!'

"The boy was unable to rise from the ground, and in a state of seeming thrall, was carried to his pallet in the house. There he lay, first silent, then groaning, when suddenly he sat up again, and with eyes staring in frightful fury, he cried out the great battle cry of the village. So loudly did he bellow that all the people of the village stopped what they were doing and came to gather about the house!

"For the next three hours, the boy continued shouting, calling out orders of flanking attacks and counter attacks, and then he shouted an order to, 'Charge!'

"Screaming in bloody shrieks (as was the custom of the Vikings on attack) the boy carried on until at last he shouted, 'We have prevailed! To the boats! To the boats! Bring the wounded and see you bear them gently.' Then he fell back, exhausted, and descended into a deep sleep that held him for three days.

"On the fourth day, Dnard awoke. He rose from his bed and walked to the harbor, and there he stood, each hour, until the sun sank into the sea.

"On the next day, he returned to the harbor to stand again. The village began to avoid him in fear, for he seemed to still be in the grip of some strange bewitchment, giving no response when spoken to, and neither speaking nor eating.

"On the sixth day, when he stood at the shore, he at last recognized the sails of his father's ships returning home. Soon he was joined by the whole village, come to receive the returning warriors.

Fig. 8: Drawing of Viking ship

"But it was not the joyous homecoming the village had expected. The boats landed and the wounded were carried off; many a brave man's body showing cuts and gashes, and some even missing limbs.

"The stretcher bearing the Chief, Ddvadajk, came ashore last and was slowly carried up to the village.

Ddvadajk lay on the very edge of death, but when the procession reached his house, he called for his son to stand beside him, and in a voice stronger than could be imagined from a man thus wounded, he told the village what had happened.

"'We were doomed. Trapped and outnumbered. I was stuck down by an enemy's axe and lay dying on the ground. Then, out of nowhere, a warrior appeared. It was my son, Dnard, and all the men saw him and heard his battle cry. With his sword raised, Dnard ran at the enemy, calling for the men to follow him. And follow they did. And fight. And our enemies were overwhelmed.' Ddvadajk paused to catch his breath and allow his wife to wet his parched lips with ale before continuing, 'At last they turned in defeat and ran, then the boy, my son, called for us to return to the boats.'

"'But he came not aboard, instead vanishing into the air. We sailed the hard days back, owing our lives to the great warrior, Dnard. I cannot explain how he came there, but I know that it was his courage and his great warrior's spirit that saved our lives.'

"'I do not think now that I will survive, but I die gladly to take up my place in Valhalla. In my place here, I leave my son. Follow him and grant him the honor due a great warrior.'"

At this, our host rose from his seat and throwing back his head, he himself let go with a cry—a great battle shout—and the one discernable word needing no translation, was the name of the boy, Dnard. In the passion of his cry, I grasped completely how important this great legend was to this chief and this people, even now, hundreds of years later.

Fig. 9: Drawing of Viking

~VIII~
Minden, Germany – July 27th, 1888

As it happened, circumstances took us some distance off our route on the return journey, and Vanya became increasingly nervous for fear we would not reach our destination in Romania in time. As we traveled one day, our coach bouncing along on a corduroy road of laid timber, I tried to while away some time with conversation.

"Vanya, are you sleeping?"

My companion did not raise his head, but opened one doleful eye and said, "Yes. That is to say, I was sleeping, or even, perhaps, that I was trying to sleep, but now, I am not," and he fetched a great yawn.

"Forgive me," I said, "but I am unable to rest with this jostling. Pray, let me learn something more of you and your life. You have told me of your wounding in the battle, and of you remarkable rescue. But what then?"

Vanya rubbed his eyes, then his whole face, briskly. "Then," he began, leaning forward, elbows on his knees, irritation with me forgotten, "I became a traveler . . . like you. I joined up with the Gypsies and traveled with a caravan."

"Yes, I had noticed your great gold earring and wondered at it. It seemed out of place for a military man. I thought it made you look like a pirate, but now I see it is a Gypsy's ring."

My mind lit with images of Vanya in the company of mysterious women and mustachioed men. "But please, you must explain to me how you came to leave the army . . . and how that was possible."

Vanya settled back on his seat, stretching out his long legs and crossing them at the ankles, "You might say I was a deserter of a sort. But then, it is not really possible for a man who is dead to desert, eh? So I should say, I think, that I simply moved on. No one pursued me, and I traveled with the Gypsies for several years.

"Then I fell in love with a beautiful woman, the daughter of the Gypsy leader, and she with me. Her father had intended that she marry one of the Roma men of the troupe, but as long as I was there, she refused," he heaved a sigh and added matter-of-factly, "so in the end, I had to leave her, to flee in the night when I heard that her father was planning to slit my throat while I slept.

"It was while I lived with the Gypsies that I saw my dead friend, Trasch again, but only in the vaporous form of a ghost. It was he who commanded me to seek out the mysteries of living and dying.

"Then later, in a dream, he came again, alerting me to you and your quest. And so I sought you out and followed you, but without identifying myself . . . ", Vanya looked very pleased with himself at this thought, " . . . until I was sure that you, too, were chosen by fate to delve into these selfsame mysteries."

So I then asked Vanya, "What have we learned in our travels, do you think?" but he turned the question back to me, saying that it was for me, as keeper of our tales to catalogue the lessons of our discoveries.

As I felt, for the most part, that I was the student in this affair, seeking understanding from whatever knowledge and guidance Vanya was gracious enough to share with me, I put aside my feeling of disappointment that he would not answer, collecting my thoughts for a moment before offering my sense of what we had encountered.

"We have seen that death can be persuaded to pass over and leave people free from their mortal fetters—at least for a time.

"We have learned that living persons can be transported in spirit from one place to another without their physical bodies, and that in the incorporate form, they can act with valor and heroism.

"We have learned that heroes can extend their power from their earthly lives to times centuries beyond, to stand in defense of their beloved homeland.

"And we know that some living souls are granted extraordinarily long lives . . . for reasons that are not yet clear to me," I trailed off, again pondering my encounter with the curiously old man, John Tars.

"So what does this all mean, then, as a collective experience?" Vanya leaned forward and grasped me by my shoulders, staring deeply into my eyes. Although I sensed in him a subtle, but almost primitive agitation, I could tell him only that it was clear that the truth lay far beyond my conventional expectations and could offer no further explanation of how this might be.

"Human life," I suggested, "is both mortal and immortal, both prosaic and divine, and rather more often than one might think, defies both science and philosophy altogether."

Vanya let go of my shoulders and slammed back on his seat once more, staring at me as though stunned. I had just voiced deeply troubling truths, the flow of which ran entirely contrary to the mainstream of accepted thought. He turned away and gazed out the window, refusing to speak further.

Hours passed in silence. We had progressed slowly along our intended route, and as night closed in, we found ourselves approaching the town of Minden, Germany at the Porte Westphalia.

Minden, we discovered, was a fairytale; a medieval town with winding narrow streets and crooked houses lining cobbled ways not wide enough to allow two horse-drawn carts to pass. The center square was dominated by two ancient structures: The nine hundred year-old Dom and The Rathaus.

I should diverge from my tale for a moment to comment on what a commodious and sensible idea I found the existence of a beer hall, a *ratskeller*, in the basement of the Minden Town Hall. Not only did the establishment serve to bring the citizenry to the town center, it provided as well an unofficial meeting place for the Mayor and the Burgers, who no doubt arranged agreements and settled disputes with exceeding good will over their foaming steins.

I was bone-weary from our bumpy and frustrating ride, and in spite of Vanya's loud protests in favor of haste, I insisted that I be allowed to take some time for a walk along the Weser River. Vanya's ill temper continued and he would not join me, so I walked out alone.

As I headed down across the wide field to the river, I heard the word *wiede* sound in my head and I did not recognize it. Then, as I came to the river bank, the voice in my head repeated *fluss*. Again I puzzled over the foreign sounds visiting upon my consciousness, whose meanings I did not know. I suspected the words were German, though I had no real knowledge of that language.

Walking along a foot path and under a bridge, the word changed to *bruke* and then, as I passed some animals grazing in the field, the words came faster, one after another, *schaffen, kuhen,* and finally, *schwiene* as I saw that a pen alongside the fence held pigs.

Fig. 10: Ratthaus

At last I caught on. The words in my head *were* German, each one, by some unknown and mystical force, naming that which I saw.

Intrigued, pleased, yes, even delighted, I walked on into the foothills of the Weser Mountains and climbed a path as *eichornchen* chased each other up and down the *baume*. I climbed to the great statue of Kaiser Wilhelm that stood beneath a pillared memorial overlooking the valley below where *denkmal* sounded in my mind.

"What a curious phenomenon," I thought, realizing, as I walked, that having these words gave me an exceedingly pleasant feeling.

Coming back into town, I strolled across the cobblestones on the square and then crossed to the ancient Dom. I entered through the huge front door and paused to give my eyes a moment to adjust to the dim light.

Other than rows of wooden benches, the structure was generally quite barren. A simple pulpit was raised above the congregation, which at the moment consisted of only one huddled old woman toward the back. I advanced several rows into the church and sat down behind her.

Although I was not a religious man, I bowed my head for some moments, sitting in silence, without any real intension of forming a prayer, my mind turning over the bits and pieces of my travels as they surfaced.

And then, I heard a voice from the pulpit.

I looked up, but saw no one, yet clearly heard words, indecipherable, in some harsh and ancient dialect.

At first, I could understand none of it; then slowly, as it had while I walked, the meaning began to come, too, flowing in through the deep and firmly-formed words. I listened intently as the voice intoned its solemn message.

The text, presumably from the Bible, related each passage, in turn, to miracles wrought by God and by Christ: parting the Red Sea, the raising of Lazarus, the loaves and fishes, and of course, the resurrection. Pausing, the voice held quiet for a few moments, then in a different cadence—words being spoken instead of words being read—it exhorted, "Do not despair of our time, nor think that God is no longer present among us. You have but to open your eyes and heart to see the miracles; the mysteries of life and death that continue, down through the ages. Go now and be glad."

Then all was silent.

I looked at the old woman who still sat, head bowed, giving no sign of having heard anything. Then, as quietly as possible, I stood up and walked out into the reflected sunlight of the late afternoon which turned the faces of the buildings to shimmering gold in the alpenglow.

~IX~
Köln, Germany –
August 4th, 1888

As we traveled the long distance south through Germany, we came to Cologne, or Köln as it was called locally, well known for the magnificent cathedral which stood at its heart. The start of the great church's construction had occurred more than four hundred years before; its completion, a mere eighty. Acres of spires soared hundreds of feet into the sky, and I had never seen a more ponderous and impressive structure, whether sacred or secular.

As I stood staring, trying to right my sense of perspective, weighed down as it was by my proximity to the *Kölner Dom's* sheer mass, it occurred to me that although its ornate decorations were meant to celebrate the awesome magnificence of God, they—and indeed, the building as a whole—evinced in my mind, an undeniable onerousness. For me, this *Cathedral de Cologne* seemed to stand in solemn judgment of human inadequacy, sinfulness and guilt, and I wondered if the labor involved in building of it must not have felt like one enormous, centuries-long act of atonement; though what great sin mankind felt guilty of, I could not name.

I wandered through the front doors, each standing at least three stories high, and continued on into the soaring vaulted interior. Here, the splendor of the stained glass windows, some taller than houses, and the intimacies of the quiet chapels and niches with their relics and statues of saints situated along the sides of great nave, conveyed what was perhaps a more sharing and forgiving feeling. In spite of its immensity, I felt that here, in its interior spaces, the *Kölner Dom* did offer some promise of protection and comfort to the trifling humans who entered to worship, or even just to look.

After spending a long time in, if not prayer, at least reverent thought before the Shrine of the Magi, I turned to exit, slowly retracing my steps beneath the great vaults of the ceiling. Once more in the narthex, I was about to pass through the great door when I noticed a number of pamphlets arrayed on a table. I pick up several and was glancing through them—one pictured the original site of the Roman fort at Köln—when another small tri-fold caught my eye.

I picked it up and scanned the title: "*Upon the Very Necessary Reasons for My Dying.*" Opening it and reading, I discovered that it was, in truth, a suicide note; a kind of confessional which ended, according to a note on the last page, with the woman who had written it fulfilling the act she foretold therein, leaping from one of the spires of the cathedral, and falling to her most horrible death.

The piece was dated August 4, 1883, and the account it contained was chilling. The woman identified herself as Liselotte Wegenteiner, aged twenty-four. She stated that she had been the school teacher in a small town outside of Köln, and in that office, on the 4th of August in 1882, she had been tending her class, when her suitor, the young lad whom she loved, but had been forbidden by her father to see, came to the window of the school and knocked.

Seeing him there, she told the children, nine in all—five boys and four girls—to tend to their copy books. She went to the front door and thinking that she did not want to chance having the children stray off, locked it. She and the young man then ran hand-in-hand into a copse of trees a short distance across the open yard where they embraced.

The young man then touched Liselotte amorously and began to remove her clothes. She looked around anxiously for fear someone should see, but there being no one, soon yielded to her lover. After they had lain together, her passion cooling, Liselotte had turned away with a growing feeling of regret and shame. This was when she noticed smoke and fire coming from the school building.

The lad, fearing discovery—fearing more that Liselotte's father would make good on his promise to do him great harm should his pursuit of Liselotte not end—bolted to his horse and rode away.

Liselotte ran to the school, struggling to cover herself as she went, but discovered that she had dropped the key and so, could not open the door. The screams from inside were horrible as the trapped children were caught in the rising flames.

Finally regaining the key at the site of the tryst, Liselotte ran back, unlocked the door and flung it open before covering her mouth and running inside. She grabbed two children by the hand and dragged them out. She turned back, reentering the building, and succeeded in finding two more.

By now, townspeople had been alerted by the smoke, and had come running. They took the children into their arms and carried them away from the inferno to safety.

Liselotte turned to enter the building for the third time just as the roof collapsed, and two large men grabbed her arms, holding her back. For many minutes, she continued to scream, shouting again and again that there remained five more children still inside.

In the end, none of those five children could be rescued, and one of the little girls who Liselotte had managed to drag from the fire—little Anna, who was six—died a few days later. Six children dead. And because no one but Liselotte knew the circumstances, she was hailed as a hero; one who had risked her life to carry the children out.

In the months that followed, Liselotte withdrew, and in time would neither leave her house nor speak with anyone. Finally, she did leave her house and traveled to Köln to pray in the small Chapel of the Sacrament just beyond the transept which housed the star-crowned Madonna of Milan, said to have miraculous powers.

It would seem, however, that no miracle was granted to Liselotte, for on August 4th of the following year, she left her note in the confessional and climbed to the high spire, from which she leapt to her death.

As dreadful as this tale was, the last line caused me to feel the chill of horror as never before, for the young woman had also written that she would repeat her death plunge each year, on August 4th, until her penance was complete; until she had leapt and died six times.

Stunned, disbelieving, I walked out onto the broad plaza in front of the cathedral. All at once, my conscious mind registered that which my sub-conscious was desperate to share; that the current month was August. With a deep sense of dread, I turned to a passerby and confirmed that the date was, indeed, the fourth.

I was by now standing in the midst of a small crowd which had begun to gather, many of them looking upward toward the spires. For a moment, I did not truly comprehend. And then, I did. And I knew.

I stood transfixed, caught like a leaf in an eddy as the crowd swelled and grew, until suddenly, a man shouted, "Look there!" and pointed at the falling figure, clearly visible, hurtling toward the ground. There was an unbearable thud, the sound of which I will take with me to my grave, and the body lay still.

The police arrived in moments and lifted the young woman's lifeless form from the pavement and placed her into their open wagon. There was unbroken silence until someone in the crowd uttered one single word which brought the hairs on my neck to a stand.

"Funf," they said. Five.

I hurried away, and finding Vanya in our chambers, begged him to come with me to the *gaststube*, where I quickly consumed the better part of two bottles of wine, speaking not a word. Vanya sat, respecting my silence, sharing the drink.

It would be three days before I could tell Vanya what I had observed.

Fig. 11: Kölner Dom

~X~
Romania – August 24th, 1888

"It is time," Vanya announced one day as we sat at breakfast. His riding cloak was draped over his knee and I knew that he was restless. Vanya was not a man to stay long in one place.

"Time for what?" I inquired, truly curious about what adventure my companion might have in mind for us next.

"To continue in haste to Romania where we will meet Father Christophus. We must leave today." Before I could react, he stood and went directly to the keeper of the inn and barked a command that horses were to be readied at once. Clearly I had no say. We were to be off, and that was that.

By ten that morning, we were well along our way. Vanya seemed to always know which road we were to follow and he led us along at a rapid rate. His uncanny sense of direction could, and did, cross uncharted territory as though it were as familiar as the village in which he had been raised. Still, I wondered what could be the cause for so much urgency.

As was often true with Vanya, I did not know what was in his mind. As was also often true, he seemed to be able to read my thoughts and soon slowed his horse to a walk. "The horses need to rest a bit, and you have questions to ask, yes?"

"Yes," I agreed. "Why such haste? Where are we going? And who is Father Christophus?

Vanya chuckled, shaking his head, and answered, "Yes, many questions! We hurry because Father Christophus is very old. We must see him before he dies and I sense that he is not well. You will find the answers to the rest of your questions in due time."

I pondered this as the horses moved us along at a walk for some minutes more, then, already urging his horse forward, Vanya laughed, "Let us now resume our more rapid pace," and tore off at a full gallop, leaving me holding on for dear life as my mount struggled to catch up.

Thus we rode for four days, crossing from Germany into Hungary, and then three more days before we crossed into Romania. Continuing into the central region known as Transylvania, we entered into a landscape which was breathtakingly beautiful. High mountains and dark green woodlands stretched for endless miles and small villages appeared suddenly in unlikely places; in hidden valleys and alongside mysterious rivers that rushed wildly by, fed by mountain snows.

We began to climb a steep trail up and up, winding along precipices which overlooked sharp valleys, clinging to stony cliffs which walled the inside of the trail while escarpments of a hundred feet or more fell away at the outer edge of the narrow shelf on which we rode; at once foolhardy and compelled. Higher and higher we climbed under the bright sun which burned through the thin air until we came to a summit; not the highest summit, as this peak was surrounded by greater peaks that stood, I would guess, six thousand feet or higher. We descended then into a gentle grassy *col*, arriving at a small cluster of stone buildings which surrounded a diminutive, but beautifully steepled church.

We drew our horses to a halt in front of a low hut with a rough wooden door that hung on huge iron hinges. Vanya marched directly to it and knocked loudly, then waited and waited as he commented over his shoulder, "Father is quite deaf. We will likely have to shout," before knocking again.

Then, with exaggerated slowness, the door was opened and a hooded figure, thin and ancient, peeked warily around it. Upon seeing who stood there, his eyes grew wide and he exclaimed, "Vanya! I have but few visitors these days and now, my great gift of God, here you stand before me!"

Father Christophus was not as old in appearance as I had anticipated. His dark hair and beard framed a face covered in wild tangles; clearly neither shaven nor shorn in many months—perhaps even years. He wore a draped black robe tied 'round the waist with a braided belt of red and gold which ended in enormous tassels, and around his neck hung a great wooden cross; so ponderously large, it caused me to wonder if that might be the cause of his persistent stoop, though I suspected the more likely cause was simply that the old man had curvature of the spine.

Upon seeing me standing behind Vanya, the holy man's face erupted in an enormous smile exposing strong white teeth behind the thicket of unkempt beard.

"And who is this that you have brought along to me?"

"This is my friend, Father," Vanya told him, stepping aside as he likewise pushed me forward, "A traveler, but no tourist. A seeker of the truth."

Father Christophus turned full to me and opened his arms to receive me in a hug, which I accepted. As he kissed me on each cheek, he said "Welcome my son, welcome, welcome." Then he turned and likewise embraced Vanya.

"Come in. Come in. Use care. The door is low," he said as he led us inside.

We followed Father Christophus into a room of the most simple sort; no more than ten feet square with a fireplace at one end and a small alcove to the side. A small table and the four chairs around it took up the greater part of the space. To the one side, there was a neatly rolled sleeping pallet, and alongside the door, under the single window, sat a desk and chair. Books were piled here and there, mostly on the floor, but a single shelf held other volumes as well. The room was in semi-darkness, as the light from the window was fading, and only a small fire burned on the hearth.

Happily for us, a large iron pot hung over the fire, bubbling fragrantly, and after Father Christophus bade us sit, he immediately served out three bowls of thick soup and placed a basket of heavy, dark bread upon the table.

"First we feed the body," he said, "before we seek nourishment for the soul," and he bowed his head in prayer.

After a shared "Amen," we ate in silence. I had the feeling that the good Father may have gone a rather long time since his last meal, because he devoured his soup noisily, quickly refilled his bowl and devoured that as well. Then he sat, contentedly waiting, until we, Vanya and I, had finished our portions. The simple meal had indeed filled in the pit of my hunger most remarkably, so it was with profound gratitude that Vanya and I again joined our host, bowing our heads in prayers of thanks.

"Amen!"

Looking up and gesturing expansively, Father Christophus faced my Russian friend, "Now, Vanya, what is it that has brought you this great distance?"

Placing his large hand on my arm, Vanya answered, "My companion has been on a quest for the inexplicable and wondrous. It is now time—for he is ready to believe—that you share with him the story of your brethren and their miracles of long ago."

We sat then and listened for more than two hours, as the sun slowly faded and candles were lit. Father Christophus went back and back in history. Back four hundred, then five hundred years, telling of the early brethren of his particular sect of Christianity—neither Roman nor Orthodox—who had retreated to this very spot, high in the mountains, to pray and seek further understanding of the messages of the Bible. And then, rolling back even further in time, he retold the story of the life of Jesus—of Jesus' relationship to man, Jesus as God's only son, Jesus as one and the same with God and the Holy Spirit. After a long time, he returned to the history of his own enclave.

When not observing times of prayer or solitude, he explained, the brothers would go down into the villages. The people of the scattered mountain hamlets were poor, but they did not know it, so isolated in these valleys were they that they knew almost nothing of the world beyond, as travelers rarely came through the region.

The brethren were among the few inhabitants of the region to actually travel, and went to the cities to visit the great scriptoriums of the churches and read the books collected there. While in the cities, they would hear of explorations and advances in science and philosophy, and when they returned, these men of faith would gather their flocks and share their adventures with the villagers who would sit, listening in wonder at the images and tales.

The good Father said proudly that, to the villagers, the most amazing stories were those of the Bible, as the wonder of God's immense creativity and love seemed to align with their own personal experiences; inhabiting the villages, living in close-knit families, and drawing their living from the earth that supported the fruit trees, vegetables, grains and live stock which sustained them. All this they understood as the love of God and the lessons of Christ made manifest.

Life they understood, but what troubled them and remained beyond their understanding was the phenomenon of death. For what did life mean in the face of death? Death could come and take away an old man who had lived well and was infirm—that was surely true. But it could also take away a man in his prime or a young, healthy woman giving birth, crushing the man who adored her, whose child she carried. And what of that child? Either losing its mother or dying with her? To lose a beloved child at any age . . . No, death was arbitrary. Death was inexplicable. Death could not, it seemed to the villagers, be something of God.

The brethren tried to explain mortality and to comfort the people by telling them about the gifts from God—the assurance of heaven and life everlasting—but although it was clear that the people tried to have faith, it was also clear that complete trust and belief escaped them.

The villagers' difficulty in attaining a state of grace—true faith in the most essential part of the Christian message; the belief in the promise of life after death, the true hallmark of faith which was essential for their salvation—tortured the good Brothers.

So it was, that Brother Ephesias began an intense study of the Scriptures, and indeed, a study of all the ancient and contemporary writings he could find. He would spend hours and hours in fasting and prayer, alone in the hut high above the monks' enclave. He spent days and days, studying, writing, and praying for guidance, without even the comfort of a fire, protected only by a bearskin blanket and his faith.

For more than two years, Brother Ephesias held himself apart, until one day in the spring, after he had been away through the harshest of winters with terrible blizzards and bitter, bitter cold, he returned and announced to the wide-eyed monks that he, Brother Ephesias, had died and had come back to life.

Knowing that Brother Ephesias would not lie, the monks were amazed, but nothing could match their wonder when he told them that he had also found the secret of resurrection; life to *mortal flesh* after death. He explained that, as with the resurrection of Christ, God had a miracle for certain other humans—physical life on earth after death.

Brother Ephesias then invited Brother Tonexum to join him and serve as witness, stating that his intention was to visit one of the villages, and there, to restore to life one who had died. God, he said, had given him strict requirements as to whom he should resurrect in the name of Christ.

So it was that the two monks traveled down the steep mountain trail into the village of Tablemum. They were, as ever, welcomed warmly, and after general greetings and various blessings, a woman stepped forward out of the crowd and told the holy men that her daughter was very ill; feverish, and calling out for her father who was away.

The Brothers retired to the home of the woman and there, found the girl. Brother Ephesias knelt and prayed, and after a long time, he rose and turned to the mother, saying with great sadness that the girl was too ill and would soon perish; going without impediment, to The Father. He prayed over the girl again, delivering last rites, and then, with Brother Tonexum, took his leave.

Brother Tonexum quietly asked his friend whether he would bring the miracle of resurrection to this poor child, but Brother Ephesias shook his head as he answered, "No, it is not God's will. This child will enter into heaven by her innocence. She needs no miraculous intervention on her behalf."

After giving what comfort they could, the two friars traveled on to the next village which was called Jestorneven. Again they were greeted with warmth and respect, and again word reached them that a villager was nearing death; this time, a very old man.

At the home of the old man, Brother Ephesias prayed, then rising from his knees, told the man's wife, "Your husband is near death. He will live only a few hours more and we will remain here at his side. After, he must not be moved for three days, for I will then return, and if God is willing, I will restore him to life."

The woman gasped, and with wide eyes and trembling hands, said she could do no such thing because her husband's body would require preparation for burial, as was the custom.

Whereupon Brother Ephesias raised his voice to her saying, "Woman, would you call forth the Lord's wrath? Do as I tell you."

Within the hour, the old man had died, after which, his wife washed him and laid him out upon the bed, crossing his arms and weighting his eyes, but she went no further with the usual preparations for his burial.

On the third day, Brother Ephesias returned and quickly asked that he be left alone in the room with the body, with only Brother Tonexum to assist him. The man's wife, his son, and his daughter rose from their stations around the bed and left quietly as Brother Ephesias knelt to pray.

After a time, the good friar began to weep, whether tears of sadness or joy, Brother Tonexum could not tell, but tears which, he noted, fell in quantity onto the old man's skin. More time passed, and Brother Ephesias went into a trance and slumped onto the floor, and when Brother Tonexum hurried to help, he discovered that Ephesias was not breathing.

Not knowing what else to do, Brother Tonexum himself knelt to pray, and after a long time, his prayers were answered as Brother Ephesias rose up, calling out to the old man, "Rise now and join me in life. Rise now and I will hear your confession."

At these words, the old man sat up blinking and asked, "Do I live? For surely I was dead."

"Yes, you now live, but you must now make your true confession and God will give you penance."

Brother Ephesias then called the man's wife and children back into the room where all three cried out with joy to see him sitting up, alive.

Ephesias addressed the old man again, "Now, before God and your family, you must make your true confession."

The old man looked wide-eyed, first turning to Brother Ephesias, and then to his family—wife, daughter and son—before his eyes returned to the face of the priest.

"But I have no confession," he said.

Brother Ephesias smiled in the kindest way and asked, "But do you not have another son who is not here?"

"No!" the old man protested, "I have no other son."

The old man's wife lowered her eyes while their son and daughter looked on, puzzled, and Brother Ephesias addressed the old man a third time, "Many years ago, you turned away a son and left him for his mother to raise alone. He has been fatherless all his life and needs to know who his father is. Go to him. Beg his forgiveness. This, you must do."

Wordlessly, the old man rose from his deathbed and went to seek out his son and the boy's mother. When he found them, he told them of the miracle of his resurrection, and told the man his son had become that he was his father, and begged forgiveness for his weakness and disregard. And he gave his son twelve pieces of gold, enough to make his life secure, and to allow his son to care for his mother who was now an old woman herself and not well.

The old man's wife went also out into the village; her purpose, to tell everyone of the miracle, and how her husband had come back to life. The village rejoiced doubly. For the old man's miracle, and for his reunion with his son, so long denied.

The villagers honored Brother Ephesias with a feast, although he insisted that he deserved no credit for what was certainly God's choice. After prayers and a shared meal, he rose from his place and said once more that God alone chose who could be granted resurrection in the flesh, and that God's will had been done.

To illustrate his point, he told the villagers the story of the young girl in Tablemum who had recently died but had not been resurrected because God accepted her directly into heaven. He explained how some would be found too sinful for resurrection, while some would be chosen to complete a task. Brother Ephesias gestured to the old man, flanked by his newly acknowledged son and the son's mother who was happily visiting with his wife and their children. The joy of the miracle, which had allowed confession, forgiveness and faith, was obvious on the family's faces as a great cheer went up.

Brother Ephesias raised his hand to quiet the crowd and once they were still, invited them to prayer. After prayers together, he reminded his flock that the mark of true belief was acceptance of Christ as the Son of God, and with that acceptance, they must also believe in the resurrection of Christ to life in the flesh, and after that, His ascension into Heaven. He admonished them to grasp faith, to take from the events they had witnessed, true and sustaining belief.

As the throng silently pondered, murmuring quietly among themselves, Brother Ephesias spoke once more in somber and reverent tones. Pointing to the old man, he said, "This man was granted resurrection to complete his life. He has done so. As with Christ, he will ascend to Heaven on the third day and you will see him no more. Let this proof of his eternal life serve as a lesson to all of you. Leave nothing of love, and reverence, or duty undone during your life, for few will be granted this great gift which you have here been privileged to witness."

On the third day, the old man could not be found. He had awakened early from his bed and gone out for a walk, but never returned to his home. It was as foretold, and the villagers held faith that the old man was now in Heaven.

Brother Ephesias then left the village, traveling on with Brother Tonexum, his companion and witness. As they traveled, Brother Ephesias repeated the miracle in village after village, bringing true faith to the people. Not all who died were allowed to rise again, and those who did inevitably had a last act of love to complete.

When the two holy men returned to their brethren, Brother Tonexum attested to the truth of what Brother Ephesias had done. Again, Brother Ephesias insisted that it was not something he had done, rather, a miracle accomplished by God for which his faith was only the instrument. He could not say how the miracle occurred, nor could he pass the gift on to another.

"Brother Ephesias lived to the very great old age of one hundred and twenty-seven years, and when he died, a special service in his memory was written," Father Christophus smiled, savoring the long story of his community's history, "and that service is repeated here every year.

"Until recently, it occasioned pilgrimages by hundreds of believers who would gather in this holy place." He sighed deeply, shaking his head, "Now, I fear that true belief has once more been lost. Few come to the service. Christ's lessons have again become only words, repeated without faith."

Fig. 12: Villages in Transylvania

~XI~
Stamm, Switzerland – September 14th, 1888

After days more travel, still desiring to keep to the high mountains, Vanya and I found ourselves now in Switzerland, having traveled across the breadth of Austria. We came first to Lucerne, and then to the little village of Stamm at the foot of Alps. Here, Vanya told me that he could stay no longer, having urgent matters to attend to, and true to the mystery of his arrival, so he departed.

But his last words to me were a warning, "Use great caution, for you risk the surrender of more than you know. Beware of all things that appear to offer life where such a gift may not be righteously given." With this, he rode away, and I was not to see him again for a very long time.

For three evenings consecutively, I had taken my supper at the *gasthaus* where I was staying. The meals were home- cooked and inexpensive, and after the weeks of travel, I was enjoying the process of settling in and becoming at least a little known in the place.

The other guests were generally a mix of travelers, merchants and tourists, as well as a goodly number of local folks who came in often enough that I had begun to recognize them, and they me.

The keeper of the house, who ran the bar at night, had begun to exchange remarks with me, asking about my travels and troubles, as barkeeps across the world are wont to do, and I had established a regular place in the room, sitting at the same table each night.

From my vantage point in a well-located corner, I could see both comings and goings. Across the room, I observed that I had something of a double in a man who came in each evening and sat in his own place, like a student assigned to a particular desk. He observed, as did I, everything with interest. But unlike me, he was very advanced in years. On several occasions in the early evening I watched him take up an ancient walking stick, gnarled and much worn on its knobby handle. With his stick, he would negotiate his way to the bar with the careful steps of a man who had perhaps suffered a damaging fall and henceforth felt insecure if each step was not placed with extreme caution. I reckoned him to be well up into his eighties or older, judging by the curve of his spine and the deeply wrinkled skin that sagged beneath his chin, despite of the gauntness of his face.

When he reached the bar—and this ritual was invariant—the barkeep would interrupt whatever he was doing, whether conversing or even drawing a beer for another patron, and immediately proceed to carefully draw a rich, dark draught for the old man who would receive it without comment and return to his table. Although I sat there each evening until the old man departed, I never saw him pay a single coin.

Now I must confess that it was not the presence of an old man in a *brauroom* that caught my attention, for such fellows seemed omnipresent in the various pubs and *gasthouses* I visited through Ireland, England and Europe.

There followed, however, a series of events involving this particular ancient fellow—events that challenged believability even beyond all that I had to this time experienced or heard. It is for this reason, the very mysterious nature of these events, even their unacceptable implications, that I attempt to write this remarkable tale.

But let me return to the sequence as it occurred. As I said, I took my dinner in the *gasthouse*, and then habitually sat over my beer for a long evening of observation. The old man was there from the first night. He, too, took his dinner, which he ate with mechanical movements of sublime disinterest before sitting, as I did, over his beer.

At about nine o'clock the first evening, a band of young men swept in with instruments—an accordion, a pipe of some sort, a drum, and a small horn—and set up chairs against the wall opposite the fireplace before commencing to play with more gusto, I felt, than was needed in the low-ceilinged *stube*. Their repertoire included dance tunes; polkas and waltzes, and other melodies of what is called *Stimmungs Musik*. Still, nothing remarkable in this.

I listened, quite enjoying this music which had its roots in a culture and time far different than anything in my own American experience, and noted that my ancient companion in the room, to whom I had not yet spoken a word, had been joined by a very beautiful young woman. She was blond, with her hair done in a traditional Swiss braid, wearing a long full skirt with a tight fitting bodice that opened revealingly beneath her long neck. I placed her age at no more than nineteen, perhaps twenty.

The old man had clearly been expecting her, and he stood to greet her with a hug, and a kiss on the cheek. Her grandfather, I surmised, or even her great-grandfather. They sat and talked, the old man quite evidently delighted, as laughter, like that between dearest friends, rose up from the table.

As I glanced over, looking more closely at the old man, it suddenly occurred to me that the girl's youthful presence must somehow be reflecting onto the old fellow, quite noticeably altering his appearance, for he now looked markedly less aged. His eyes shone, his cheeks had bloomed with color, and even the folds of skin beneath his chin seemed, minute by minute, to grow tighter.

He moved his arms about as I watched, speaking and gesturing with surprising animation. Then, to my great astonishment, he suddenly stood and, offering his hand to the young lady, escorted her onto the dance floor. Instead of hesitation, and with no sign of distaste, her face fairly glowed, her broad smile conveying nothing by the utmost affection.

As the music swirled into a fast-paced polka, the unusual couple stepped smoothly into the midst of the other dancers, twirling and leaping around the small dance floor. With sure-footed high-stepping and, indeed, a great deal of flourish, the old man, who now was standing straight and beaming down at his lovely young partner, led her 'round and 'round. When the dance came to an end, the two were unmistakably swept away in their delight as they returned to their table.

They joined two or three more dances, each as energetic as the last, and then, as the band played its final slow waltz, they held each other closely, even—dare I say it?—amorously. The girl looked even more radiant than when she had arrived, and the old man—perhaps I should correct myself—the *man* who now held her looked darkly handsome, no longer ancient, and if pressed, I would have said more like a man, perhaps in his thirties.

Adding to my bewilderment, I observed that no one took any note of the phenomenon I had observed.

Indeed, all the other guests either looked on with blank and unchanged expressions or looked away, seeming a bit embarrassed. After the couple left, I took myself to my room where I could not sleep for revisiting what I had seen and wondering at it all.

Had I misperceived the old man, or perhaps been deceived by the youthfulness of his energy and movement? And who were they together, this man and woman? By the end of the evening, I would have said they were young lovers, but how could that be?

Each of the following evenings, the scene repeated itself. The old man, hunched and sickly in appearance, would greet his beautiful young companion. After the third night, I got up the courage to ask the bartender who they were.

At first, hesitating to answer, he asserted that it was not something that people in the town cared to talk about. When I pressed him further, he reluctantly told me that the old man had come into town some years before; a stranger who took up residence but had never spoken about himself or told where he came from.

This stranger had refused to pay for either rent or services of any kind, and, the barman added, glancing toward the old man and lowering his voice even more, could look at a person with such menace that none dared to even try to collect their fees or, God forbid, to turn him out. As for the girl, the barman would say only that she came from a very old family of the region and was the granddaughter of the Baron and Baroness Von Heutle who had died many, many years before.

After a stay of several days, I decided to move on. I traveled to Austria, to a small village on the border of Italy, called Dorf Tyrol. I spent several weeks there, helping to harvest grapes from the abundant vineyards until once more, I became restless and decided to move on.

Without a clear plan in mind, but with an inner pull that guided me, I returned to Stamm, to the same *gasthaus* where I had stayed before.

On the night of my arrival, I was surprised to find the old man absent from his table and inquired of the barkeep who remembered me and was therefore willing to speak a little.

He told me in hushed tones that the old man was in mourning, and added, his eyes darkening with obvious dread, that the old man and the young girl had, not long ago, quarreled loudly and angrily. She had run out of the *gasthaus*, her face contorted in an expression which the barman said he could only describe as terror.

A few days later, the beautiful young companion fell gravely ill, and soon after, died of a mysterious malady, displaying symptoms like those of plague. There was, however, the barman noted, no other incident of plague in the region.

As I listened, I felt a deep sorrow, as if I myself were grieving once more for my own sweet wife, and for my parents, my brother, and indeed, for all who die. I took to bed early, but passed a sleepless night.

It was the very next evening that the old man was back, looking, if such a thing were even possible, older than before, and even more enfeebled. When the music began, he had no companion, and sat huddled at his table, shrinking back into the dark. There was about him a gloom so palpable I thought that surely he could not live.

Drawn to him in the spirit of shared grieving, I approached his table where, with an unenthusiastic move of his hand, he invited me to join him. When he did not speak, I introduced myself and told him of my recent losses, thinking to express mutual sympathy. He nodded dismissively and made no reply.

We sat in silence for several long minutes. I rose to leave saying "May you be well." He replied, "And you also." As I stepped away he spoke again.

"This may be the end," he said, and the fear I felt for his mortality seemed to cling to every word. Then there was silence, save for the rattle of his labored breath, until I thought I heard him say one more word, "unless . . . "

He spoke no more, and at last, I again wished him well, excused myself, and returned to my own table.

Only a short time had passed when a woman entered the room, cloaked and hooded so I could not tell if she were young or old. She went directly to the old man's table where she sat, pulling back her hood to allow long black hair to cascade like polished ebony down her back.

By the light of the candle on the table, it was easy to see that this was a rare beauty of a girl; very young, with a lovely profile which was fair and fine in its features.

This young and presumably innocent girl leaned over to the wizened old man and whispered something in his ear. As she drew back, I saw the old man nod, a gesture I took to be his answer, one undoubtedly in the affirmative. In that instant, the old, hooded eyes lit up as I had seen them do before. And as the music swelled, the old man stood, helped this new lady take off her cloak, then extended his hand most gallantly before leading her to the dance floor. As before, when they began to move together, the undeniable transformation began and the old man began growing younger.

Crossing to the bar, I inquired of the barman, "Who is this new maid with the old man?"

The bartender replied in a voice filled with sadness, "She is Thomasina, daughter of our Mayor."

It is, I think, most fortunate that I recorded all this, and carefully dated the entries; the year of that note being 1888. For years afterward, I continued to travel, finally settling in East Anglia, Africa where I resumed my practice of medicine among the native population.

When Vanya had taken his leave of me, he had spoken a warning, then added, "You now know the answer. You have only to see and recognize it."

I often awoke in the night, or found myself distracted during the day, by the recollection of the strange phenomena I had observed on my travels; most especially, by what I had witnessed in Stamm. Nothing in my life, nor in my medical experience could explain the reversed aging process I had witnessed in that *gasthaus*.

Reviewing all that I had experienced again and again over the years, the answer, the central meaning of it, still eluded me. True, I had found direction and inspiration, and even enough peace inside my soul to return to the practice of medicine. Also true, I have since ending my travels done some small good in tending the sick and facilitating cures and healing, where and when I could. But never have I succeeded in bringing all of it together; never finding the answer to the question which drove me to my travels.

What is the meaning of our meager lives when death is always the victor?

Fig. 13: Statue at Stamm (Photo taken in 2010 by Roper)

~XII~
Stamm, Switzerland – June 12th, 1938

The Return

For over forty years, my experiences—most especially the events in Stamm—so plagued my mind that I determined I must go back. I must return to that place, to see it again, and reviewing those events, possibly to discover more about the odd happenings and their meaning, or to somehow reach back in my own mind to make sense of it all.

Since I found myself in rather remarkable health for a man of nearly eighty, full of vigor and not at all impeded in my movements, I determined to embark now on a new round of traveling. After several brief stops along the way, I found my way back to that selfsame *gasthous* which continued to be operated by the same family; in fact, by the son and daughter of the old owner I had known.

I spoke to the son at his station behind the bar, asking after his father and passing the time with pleasantries until I felt it appropriate to ask about the old man. The change was instantaneous. His expression shifted from garrulous to tight-lipped, and judging that I would get no more from him, I retired to the same corner table I had occupied so many years before.

As I sat there, dreaming over my *sauerbraten*, I was suddenly startled to see an old man—indeed, *the* old man—who by now must be at least one hundred and twenty years of age, slowly approaching the corner table across the room. As I caught his eye, his face lit with a delighted smile of recognition. He bade me come over, then clasped my hand warmly, saying, "Good to see you, old friend! Sit. Sit down."

I sat, in large part because I feared that my legs would give way if I did not. As you might imagine, I was astonished . . . that he recognized me, at the warmth of his greeting certainly, but most of all, that he was still living.

Searching my face, he spoke the thoughts which were even then rising to the surface in my own mind, "You are little changed."

Before I could comment further, he was joined, as he had been so many years before, by a beautiful young woman, surely no older than twenty years, with long black hair and the same petite features that I had carried in my mind for years.

I was frozen. Struck dumb.

As I sat with them, literally unable to make myself move, I could see that already the old man had begun his transformation, and as the girl sat down at the table, my heart clutched again when I heard him speak her name.

"Thomasina," he whispered, "you are as beautiful today as ever you have been."

That evening, after I returned to my rooms and retired to my bed, I found myself overcome with despair. I felt corrupted, violated, filled with great sadness for the girl, Thomasina; but deeper than that, I felt a great sadness overspreading myself and indeed, my whole life. Still, I could not name what the sadness was.

For Thomasina had been aglow with youth and beauty, smiling and laughing, and of course, whirling about the dance floor in the arms of her handsome, *young* and vital partner. She was, it appeared, in no way distressed by her lot as companion to the old man, attending him as the magic of her reflected vitality transformed him, restoring his youth again and again.

But no, I realized in that moment, that I had it wrong. It was not she who transformed him, but he who transformed her. She was kept young by his power, and through that power, he drew out just enough youth to somehow enliven and sustain his own existence.

By what arrangement, by what bargain was this accomplished? How long could these two lives continue this limbo; this caricature of life?

The more I pondered, the greater my sense of sorrow, until suddenly, the old man's remark to me burst open the doors of my own mind and the seeds of my disaffection spilled forth.

"You are little changed," he had said.

With an odd feeling in my chest as though my heart had suddenly been sucked dry, hollowed out like an eggshell and about to be crushed by the intake of my own breath as I gasped, I was thrust hard against the truth and enormity of that one simple statement. For it was quite true: I was little changed.

Although I had first met the old man when I was approaching forty, it was now that many years later, yet I was not old. I had aged only slightly in appearance, my hair now lightly flecked with gray, my stance bent not at all, and my energy very much what it had always been; likely even a bit more vibrant since throwing off the dark mantle of depression I had borne during my first years as a traveler.

I had not been sick a single day since that time, in spite of tending the sick as one epidemic of contagion after another devastated the villagers with whom I lived and worked.

And work I did, often seventeen-hour days or longer, sleeping very little in times of crisis that sometimes lasted for weeks on end. It was nothing for me to work thus and then, for relaxation, to set out at a run and visit from one village to another.

I could, and often did, join the young men in sport, and I could dance long into the night around fires of celebration for marriages and great hunts, throwing myself into the drinking and dancing like the strongest of the younger men.

Did I have a link with the old man also? One of which I had heretofore been unaware? I could not think how that could be possible as I had offered him only a few moments of companionship and withheld censure and judgment of the strange things I had seen. Still, I alone acknowledged him in his grief when all the others averted their faces.

Thomasina's obligation was clear. I had seen her whispering with the old man and had witnessed the spectacular consequences of their contract. As well, I had seen Thomasina's predecessor living in the thrall of the same indenture, and learned of her dreadful end soon after a vicious argument. A request, perhaps, for a change of terms denied?

As these realizations came to me, I found that I now knew the source of my sadness. Thomasina had been allowed her youth for many years, but she was a slave to that bargain which constrained her and everything in her life. She remained young while others around her grew old. She was denied her family, denied even love, because she was committed to one who could give her neither. Someone feared and avoided by society as a whole, was, in fact, her whole society. She would have beauty forever, but to what good? What was the value of life under such circumstances?

I realized in that moment that my own life had often felt similarly empty. I had never remarried. Even after I had thought myself in love with another, quite lovely, woman, when I saw after a few years that she was changing, becoming older, becoming tired, losing her hold on her physical beauty, I had allowed whatever love I had for her to simply fade away.

I had cared deeply for many of the villagers, but my closest friends had sickened in the plagues or died of natural causes as they aged, and so I was alone. As I realized the full truth of it, a cry broke from my throat, and I sat up in my bed, trembling.

It was then that I made my resolution: I would speak to Thomasina and show her how she had been deceived; how the old man had played upon her vanity, draining her of the very purpose of her youth and beauty. She had been robbed of her proper gift, and her ability to give joy and life had instead become only a mirage; a cold reflection of the living thing.

The next evening when Thomasina came into the barroom and strode toward the old man's table, I rushed at her and grabbed her arm, saying, "Please. Please, you must listen. You must hear me and see what you are giving up in your impure covenant with this old man."

She struggled to pull her arm from my grasp, but I held firm. Then, as one, our eyes were pulled toward the old man who neither stood nor advanced toward us, though the look of rage upon his face was terrible to see, and indeed, I could feel it, like cold fingers of an evil fog, wrapping around my person.

Thomasina renewed her struggles and at last twisted free of my grasp, falling upon the floor and shouting, "Be damned and let me alone! Can you not see that you kill me?"

She quickly got to her feet and ran across the floor, throwing her arms around the old man, her tears streaming down her face, her voice wailing as she repeated over and over again, "Forgive me! Oh please, please, forgive me!"

The old man patted her head with a bony hand, then lifted one finger and pointed it at me.

"I have counted you my friend, but no more. No more." And lowering his hand, he gently stroked Thomasina's cheek, and bent to her, and softly kissed her mouth.

I watched as her tears subsided and the old man's lips began to turn rosy, losing their grey pallor, the bloom spreading across his face. I watched as Thomasina's smile returned, then I turned and withdrew.

God help me, I had accomplished nothing.

~XIII~
Rome, Italy – July 14th, 1938

By the next morning, my bags were packed and loaded on the coach, and I departed Stamm and began my travel south to Rome. Even before I had fully awakened, I felt the ache in my bones.

By the time I reached Rome, the journey had taken its toll on me, and I found it necessary to spend many days sitting in the sun, seeking warmth that somehow never quite warmed me.

Within a few weeks I had aged years. My hair had turned completely white and was becoming thin. So, too, was my skin losing its color, turning sallow and increasingly covered with brown spots. Even the owner of the pension at which I was boarding became concerned, asking if he might contact a physician to look in on me and remarking that I did not look at all well.

My condition worsened, but though I had sought the aid of two renowned physicians, I could gain neither helpful diagnosis nor useful advice. I was wearing out, they said, and reminded me of my age, which was in this year a full four-score.

I did not die then, as at first I thought I would, but gained back a little strength in the warm Italian sun.

When I left East Anglia some months before, to travel to Stamm, I had intended to return to Africa, but as that became clearly impossible, I wrote to my assistant and requested that he send me the folios of notes from my earlier travels. Since receiving these, I have put to use my remaining time in the recording and clarifying of this record, and also in visiting the great works of art in this city, as well as the magnificent ruins of antiquity. Though ancient, all these things seemed to me to be glowing with present beauty, everlasting energy, and perhaps even divine meaning.

How Vanya found me in Rome, I do not know. He approached me as I sat gazing at the Coliseum and sat down on the stone beside me.

"Hello, old friend," he said. He was now very old, and only the powerful light in his dark eyes still held the passion by which I would have known him anywhere.

"Have you found the answer?" He asked the question, but seemed to expect no reply.

Vanya and I continued to walk together about the city most days over the next few weeks, seeing the wonders, and sitting in the sun. But it soon became apparent that my strength was not improving, but failing, and

I stayed in my room where Vanya would come and sit with me. I held onto the hope that I might rest enough, regain strength enough, to go once more and sit in the piazza.

~XIV~
Rome –
October 30th, 1940

In these most recent days, I feel my strength ebbing more rapidly and I am increasingly certain that I will not live out the year, nor ever even quit my bed. Vanya comes, but less often. It is hard for him to sit and do nothing

I am nearly eighty-two, but look, it seems to me, even older. It is difficult not to draw the comparison to the vigor and vitality I possessed prior to my last visit to Stamm. I am severely bent, barely able to walk, and then, only shuffling about my small apartment with a slow gait, assisted by a stick as gnarled as my hands. The years, once so kind, have now turned upon my body with a vengeance.

I sleep a great deal, and am comforted by marvelous dreams. At times, they play before me like great canvasses of moving pictures, glorious in their colors. I re-experience events as if they were just now happening; the great experiences of my life—the kilted clansmen, the knights mounted on their chargers with colors streaming, the brave Vikings rallying in one great charge to drive off their attackers before dashing to make their escapes in their strange and ferocious boats.

I see Christina with flowers in her hair, dancing and dancing, with all the village swept up in wild and joyful celebration. All of them, all of the stories appear before me.

These days, the stories bring with them a sense of connectedness. I see them as linked together; my whole journey, a quest. I am aware that I have been allowed to experience a pattern of guided discovery and revelation, and realize that these encounters were not just my random wanderings, rather, a guided tour of physical evidence reaching well beyond the limits of everyday human existence, and even mortality.

For this purpose, I was granted a life of miracles, begun with my induction into the Clan Farquhar—my clan—and the gift of the dagger, my prized possession, kept, even now, at my bedside. Miracles which continued with the discovery of powerful forces, of life and heroism, of family and celebration; each one standing in counterpoint to the flow of time and the human lives flowing, for the most part, with it.

Some nights my own memories visit me like recitations of great ballads, of folk tales, each being part and parcel with the history and legends of all human existence.

But on other nights, my dreams take another slant, coming as formless beauty that I watch behind my eyes; blues and golds, ruby and emerald hues of the most exquisite kind. So marvelous are these visions that I begin to feel their meaning as true joy itself.

And then I begin to see that the colors are not always formless. They become more and more perceptibly a visage, an image, with features—a face—but not a human face. Not the face of any single living thing I have known, but the face of all life-fullness and beauty; the face of all art and all generosity and mercy.

I know it now in my heart, that this is the face of love.

I have heard the voice which speaks to me, saying, "Now see what you have sought. Gaze deeply without gazing and see all meanings revealed just as the universe has intended. Look on the dancing and the flowers and the heroes and the miracles and you will see how life and death are revealed; in all creation, in all destruction, in all wonder and love, in all the gifts of life and the truths of human mortality. In these, you will see the face of God."

Hearing this, I was filled with a great and sudden rush of understanding and fulfillment. I felt that I had completed my journey, and that I was whole.

The voice spoke to me again and said, "You may let go now, for you have found eternal life. For all those who complete their mission of love will die with Life's blessing, and will receive the gift of eternal peace.

"Woe to those who live lives in anger and mistrust and greed. Woe to those who have created no beauty and have experienced no selfless love, for they die incomplete and their dying is forever.

"But those who have loved life, indeed, given their life to understanding life's meaning, gain peace and fulfillment for all eternity."

I believe my journal is complete. I am thankful and content, accepting of my miracles, and prepared for where my next travels take me.

I sign this, my last entry, in Rome, October 31st, the same day as of my birth, eighty-two years ago.

Join our *Reader-Get-A-Reader* Program

Earn cash dividends by referring friends who order

Tales of the Traveler

1. Register for **Reader-Get-A-Reader** at the author's blog site:
   www.garroper.com
2. Invite your friends to order *Tales of the Traveler* and be sure they mention your name.
3. Receive $1 for each referred sale, (checks to be mailed annually.)

- Note: novels, excerpts, articles on writing, poetry and essays—are available at the blog site (www.garroper.com) with an interactive bulletin board for reading comments and leaving your own.

Other works by Gar Roper, Ph.D.

Hidden Grace: The story of a young girl's horrendous abuse in foster homes and her journey through an unconventional psychotherapy to her triumphant recovery.

Deadly Hypocrisy—Brenna Should Have Died: A sophisticated detective novel featuring the pursuit of truth through psychotherapy and detective genius. An Ackerman/Savantro Novel. Publication date: (Fall 2013)

Deadly Identity—The Burden of Success: An LA doctor fakes his own death to escape the burden of his shallow success only to find that he has been implicated in a rape and abduction…and ends up being sought for murder. The second novel in the Ackerman/Savantro series. Publication date: TBA.

Deadly Intensions—Careful What You Wish For: The death of her husband in an airplane crash leaves Julia Hanson-Baquar, not grieving, but celebrating her new wealth from life insurance and new freedom for herself and her son. But now she is a suspect and must prove the crash was an act of terror… and one that her husband was himself plotting. The third novel in the Ackerman/Savantro series. Publication date: TBA.

23866095R30094

Made in the USA
Charleston, SC
07 November 2013